Prais

"A compelling […] Smythe's *A Town* […] lays bare WWII histories of cruelty, connection, and the bright flame of repair and healing that persists into our present day. Read this powerful, moving story of a young woman coming to terms with the past, and confronting our contemporary inequalities, for its clarity and urgent call for reckoning."

—Elise Levine, *Say This* and *This Wicked Tongue*

"The epigraph of Karen Smythe's novel *A Town with No Noise* is a gorgeous poem by Derek Walcott, which alludes to stories hidden in plain sight. Smythe's narrative wends through deceptively bucolic small-town Ontario, then Toronto, then northern Ontario, to arrive, finally, at the devastating story of a Jewish girl and her family in Nazi-occupied Norway. In this skilful intertextual weave of fiction and true history, the reader is shocked and moved to come upon a past in Europe that Smythe's characters—in Canada—would prefer to forget. Smythe's protagonist Samara has taken herself on a journey of revelation and remembrance, a journey that will make of her a writer: a healer and mender. And Karen Smythe has written this story: her novel is a captivating and brave achievement."

—Dawn Promislow, *Wan*

"Karen Smythe is a brilliant and insightful observer of her character's inner lives, and *A Town With No Noise* is no exception. Smythe is a master at articulating tension between Samara and J., between their expectations and the reality that hides behind the facade of Upton Bay, and Samara's discoveries of certain character's pasts. Smythe's descriptions are gorgeous and poetic, her pacing deft and precise. A beautiful novel that I couldn't put down."

—Danila Botha, *Things that Cause Inappropriate Happiness*

"In her brilliant experimental novel *A Town with No Noise*, Karen Smythe unveils the secret histories of two towns separated by time and geography — one in contemporary Ontario, one in Occupied Norway. It explores profound questions that are especially relevant today: What is true empathy? Who deserves our compassion?

With its inventive layering of a fictional narrative with footnotes, a transcription of a recording, a play, journalism, and historical details, the novel invites us to question how history is written, remembered, and forgotten, and to listen to the stories of others. *A Town with No Noise* will surprise, move, and push you to see the world differently, as only the best fiction can."

—**Kasia Jaronczyk,** *Voices in the Air* and *Lemons*

A TOWN WITH NO NOISE

Copyright © Karen Smythe 2025
All rights reserved

Palimpsest Press
1171 Eastlawn Ave.
Windsor, Ontario. N8S 3J1
www.palimpsestpress.ca

Printed and bound in Canada
Cover design and book typography by Ellie Hastings
Edited by Aimée Parent Dunn
Cover image: *Stadt am blauen Fluss* (1910) by Egon Schiele.

Palimpsest Press would like to thank the Canada Council for the Arts and the Ontario Arts Council for their support of our publishing program. We also acknowledge the assistance of the Government of Ontario through the Ontario Book Publishing Tax Credit.

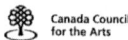  

LIBRARY AND ARCHIVES CANADA CATALOGUING IN PUBLICATION

TITLE: A town with no noise : a novel / Karen Smythe.
NAMES: Smythe, Karen, 1962- author
IDENTIFIERS: Canadiana (print) 20250182939
Canadiana (ebook) 20250182947

ISBN 9781990293924 (SOFTCOVER)
ISBN 9781990293979 (EPUB)
SUBJECTS: LCGFT: Novels.
CLASSIFICATION: LCC PS8587.M994 T69 2025 | DDC C813/.54—DC23

A Town With No Noise

a novel

KAREN SMYTHE

This book is a work of fiction. References to historical events, real people, or real places are incorporated as footnotes but are not meant to comprise historical research and therefore are part of the work of fiction. Other names, characters, places, and events are products of the author's imagination, and any resemblance to actual events or places or persons, living or dead, is entirely coincidental.

For G; always, for G.

"Think of the people who go to the market for food: during the day they eat; at night they sleep, talk nonsense, marry, grow old, piously follow their dead to the cemetery; one never sees or hears those who suffer, and all the horror of life goes on somewhere behind the scenes. Everything is quiet, peaceful, and against it all there is only the silent protest of statistics; so many go mad, so many gallons are drunk, so many children die of starvation. . . And such a state of things is obviously what we want; apparently a happy man only feels so because the unhappy bear their burden in silence, but for which happiness would be impossible. It is a general hypnosis. Every happy man should have someone with a little hammer at his door to knock and remind him that there are unhappy people, and that, however happy he may be, life will sooner or later show its claws, and some misfortune will befall him—illness, poverty, loss, and then no one will see or hear him, just as he now neither sees nor hears others. But there is no man with a hammer, and the happy go on living, just a little fluttered with the petty cares of every day, like an aspen-tree in the wind—and everything is all right."

—*Anton Chekhov, "Gooseberries"*

This page is a cloud between whose fraying edges
a headland with mountains appears brokenly
then is hidden again until what emerges
from the now cloudless blue is the grooved sea
and the whole self-naming island, its ochre verges,
its shadow-plunged valleys and a coiled road
threading the fishing villages, the white, silent surges
of combers along the coast, where a line of gulls has arrowed
into the widening harbor of a town with no noise,
its streets growing closer like print you can now read,
two cruise ships, schooners, a tug, ancestral canoes,
as a cloud slowly covers the page and it goes
white again and the book comes to a close.

—*Derek Walcott*

Part 1

SATURDAY

I am driving J. through the trees.

It is hot, humid, and my skirt has ridden up high on my thighs, which are stuck to the cracked black leather of the car seat. J.'s is tilted as far back as it will go; he is lying nearly flat, with one pillow underneath him and another behind his head, gazing up through the open sunroof that lost its glazed panel years ago. He is smiling when I glance at him. At a red light, exhaust from other engines begins to fill up the cabin, as J. calls it—because he feels like he is flying on these trips, these runs, as we call them.

We tour the valley on the road that winds around mansions set well back from the street. Downtown shrinks behind us as we approach the curving expressway to head north, where the traffic will eventually thin out. The trees become fewer and fewer as we snake our way to mid-town. I stop at a suburban bakery, where I pick out two slices of Black Forest cake, J.'s favourite, which we'll eat later, with tea, on the balcony of my apartment.

I get back in the stifling car and start driving home.

"What do you see now, J.?"

"Gray. No, it's slate. A light slate colour."

"Anything else?"

"Not sure."

It is getting late and J. sounds tired. The pain medication he takes makes him drowsy; it's stronger than Tylenol 1 but not as strong as OxyContin—something in between, the pharmacist said when I picked up the prescription, showing her my ID as well as J.'s. She almost didn't give me the bag. When I told her J. was in the parking lot, that she could go out there if she wanted to, to make sure his face matched the photograph on his health card, she sighed and handed it over. I signed the logbook and she rang me through.

"Close your eyes and rest a little, J."

"I don't want to miss the moon."

"It's probably too cloudy to see it tonight. Close your eyes, J."

But I know he won't.

I'm hoping the clouds don't mean rain, even if it would cool off the air. The tarp covering the sunroof blew off last night despite the bungee cords I hooked through the windows. I'll have to remember to buy another one for our trip tomorrow.

J. once had his own car, an old, pale-yellow Corolla, but his ex-roommate Shawn had taken it in lieu of rent owed, when J. moved out. I suppose Shawn inherited the parking tickets, too; J.'d had a collection on the dash that he'd never been able to pay, but he didn't worry about the fines because his licence plates—borrowed from a friend—were for New Brunswick. Tickets don't stick to out-of-province plates, said this friend, laughing, as if you'd be a fool to think people carried responsibility for their actions around with them, like luggage.

J. is nearly twenty-seven but hasn't given up on becoming a star. He just needs the right band, he says. "That's the trouble with being a drummer—you need other people to help make the music." And J. isn't much good at getting along with people, or at fitting in; he's a loner, like me, which is probably what attracted me to him in the first place.

Tomorrow, we pack up and head to Upton Bay, where J.'s grandparents live. I've never been there, but I am going to be writing an article about the place for a friend who freelances; Nick has too much work to write it himself, even though he tells me it will be an easy piece. We will be staying with J.'s grandparents, because even modest bed-and-breakfasts in town charge more than my fee would cover. Unlike J., who seems to have no concerns about his own debts, I'm still paying off the student loans I took to supplement my scholarship, so being able to stay with his family is a bonus.

Nick says he's looking for a brief descriptive piece only, "to promote tourism in the area." I'm supposed to feature the young entrepreneurs "who are transforming the town's economy via the maturing wine industry." He thinks I will find more than enough information to write the article. This is my first writing assignment, and if I do a decent job, I might get others. My boss at the café made me co-manager last year, and I appreciate the raise that came with it, but I'm bored with pouring coffee for a living. My mother thinks I can do better, with my degree, but it is only a BA. Everyone has a BA these days; it's almost what a high school diploma used to be.

J. didn't even graduate from high school. He told me his grandfather Otto paid for him to attend a private school, but J. was kicked out in his final year for smoking in class, and he never went back. (Otto didn't find out for years.) Apparently, Otto would pay for J. to go to university as a mature student, too, if he'd only settle on a real career and stop this musician nonsense.

J. was named after his father, but when he was a child, his parents started calling him J.J., short for John Jr. He and his father were never close; then after the divorce, J. moved away with his mother, and they grew even more distant. At fifteen he decided to drop the extra J. He's not spoken to his dad in over ten years.

"There!" J. startles me out of my thoughts. "There it is! See that, Sam?"

When I glance up, I see the glow of a waning gibbous moon before stratus clouds cover it again.

Now I know it will rain for sure, not only because of the clouds, but because the back of my head is starting to hurt. My brain makes me a human barometer: low air-pressure systems will trigger a migraine, nine times out of ten.

I adjust the pillow behind my back, which is also gibbous, slightly curved, scoliotic. Not enough for surgery, the paediatrician told my mother, but enough to keep me off the sports teams, the uneven bars, and the runways, ha ha ha. That's why I became a runner, for a while—it was something I could do by myself, with no equipment and no other people.

I pull in next to the house I've lived in for five years now and rub my neck before getting out to help J. make the voyage up the stairs.

I—we, I mean; J. and me—we live northwest of the university on the second floor of an old semi-detached house, with an art-store parking lot beside it. (I'd never be able to afford this place if it weren't for my landlord Tim, who lives downstairs; he takes care of the house for his wealthy great aunt, who has a sentimental attachment to the home she grew up in, and she keeps our rent very, very low.) The store manager next door lets me park overnight for free as long as I move the car before 8:00a.m., Monday through Saturday. On those days I set my alarm for 7:00a.m., so I can find a spot on the street before they fill up for the day. I used to go back to bed then, since my preferred hours at the café are early afternoon to evening, but ever since J. moved in with me, I've been using the mornings for walks, just to have some time for myself. I'm not like J., who can't stand his own company for long. I crave solitude the way some people crave chocolate—no, the way I craved water after I'd get home from a run, back in my student days.

I usually cover the morning shift at the café on Sundays because the tips are good (customers are especially grateful for their caffeine, it seems, after a Saturday night out), but I've taken the next few days off to get this article done. J. says Upton Bay is aptly named because it's uppity, which I'd already gathered from what I've read online; a tourist's comment I came across on a travel website praised the enforcement of town bylaws that forbid loitering on its streets: "Plus there are no homeless people panhandling, which is such a relief!" wrote Amy S. As for me, every time I see a police officer in Toronto telling homeless people to move along, I think, *Where? Where are they supposed to go?*

J. has told me a little about his family background: his grandfather's name is Otto Hermann Sommerfeld, but J. calls him Pop. He and his wife Grete emigrated from Germany to Canada as farm labourers, in the early fifties. Otto owned hotels in Upton for years, and as soon as J.'s grandmother dropped dead, he married one of the housekeeping staff.[1]

---

1 Otto and Shelley had been sneaking off to guest rooms for over a year before Grete died, which the family doesn't know.

J. won't mind seeing Pop again, he says, but he doesn't want his father to find out he is in town. I don't know what went on between them while J. was growing up, and I've never asked; but based on his mood whenever he mentions his dad, it must have been ugly.

SUNDAY

The drive to Upton Bay so far is tedious. Traffic keeps stalling—the on-ramps along the highway feed in more cars than the road has room for. I smell rotting foliage, too, whenever we're stopped: the scent of sodden, browning grass in the ditch, warmed by the sun after heavy rain, is rising up and streaming into the car. It's a wet summer scent that makes me uneasy; it reminds me of my childhood. When I was growing up near Sudbury and still too young to stay home alone when school ended for the year, I'd be sent to stay at Lift-the-Latch Lodge, where my grandmother cleaned in exchange for tips and room and board. The lodge was on a murky lake with bullrushes and weeds instead of a beach; during storms, the roof of the cabin I shared with my grandmother leaked, and the room became a sauna once the clouds disappeared and heat seeped from the loose black shingles into the wet, wooden ceiling. I would appreciate a breeze about now.

    J. is asleep beside me. He needs more sleep than anyone I have ever known. J. used to stay up all night and sleep all day, like a raccoon, and then he got sick and was barely able to move, no matter how much sleep he got. It took a long time to diagnose. Doctors asked if he was gay (internal fistulas) or a drug addict (he looked that bad); his ankles and wrists had swelled to three times their normal size, but rheumatoid arthritis was ruled out. It was serious enough to knock twenty-five pounds off his body and the colour out of his face, cheekbones protruding from his formerly full visage like a prisoner on a weeks-long hunger strike.

A surgeon was assigned to his case. "If tissue won't heal, it has to be removed," he said, and afterwards told me he had "cut out" the problem in J.'s intestine. When the fourth specialist J. saw figured out the mystery disease—Crohn's, an autoimmune disorder; nothing contagious or related to any drugs J. might have taken—they said the surgery had been a mistake, a medical no-no. It made J.'s recovery lengthy, painful, and medically complicated. He had to be re-hospitalized and fed with an enteral tube. And then he crashed.

Tubes in his kidneys, his lungs, and his esophagus kept him alive for two months; every major organ had shut down once the sepsis from an internal ulceration started spreading. J. wasn't supposed to survive after the switch was turned off. I was not next of kin, and I'd been dating J. for only a few weeks by then, but I had no contact information for J.'s father (and his mother is dead); so I fought to postpone the doctors' decision, to give me time to track down John Sommerfeld.

When J. came to, the exhilaration of seeing him take his first independent breath not only vindicated me, but made me feel permanently bonded to him, somehow. It wasn't that I expected or even hoped we'd stay together; it was more as if I'd become responsible for keeping J. alive, and after a while J. seemed happy to remain "kept."

J. soon donned an artificially healthy look from the steroids, with a rounded moon face and an increased appetite that caused rapid weight gain, which covered the atrophied musculature of his legs and arms. The ongoing treatment kept J. revved up twenty-four seven. He couldn't sleep no matter how tired he was, and his mind would not stop—nor would he stop talking in a manic stream of ideas and enthusiasms that I couldn't keep up with. It was like living on stage with Robin Williams, I would say, when asked about the early days when J. came to live with me, several months ago. He is better now, and he's losing the fluids he'd been retaining, but the medication withdrawal process, a gradual tapering off, is making him feel tired again.

After his discharge, J. wasn't strong enough to be on his own, so he moved in with me, and I felt as if I'd suddenly become his mother. I am trying to let go of that feeling, but J.'s response to his circumstances so far, something like a grateful dependence, isn't helping. When I picked up his only belongings from the place he'd been sharing with a roommate—two black garbage bags full of clothes that he has yet to unpack—I saw a large sack of dried lentils on the kitchen counter.

"Someone once told J. he could live cheaply on lentils," the roommate said. "So he spent ten bucks on that bag of beans. It's been sitting there for as long as I can remember." I declined to take it with me.

The next day I went to Honest Ed's and bought sets of T-shirts and sweatpants for J. to wear during his recovery: easy on, easy off. A temporary wardrobe, I thought, because everything about J. is temporary—or used to be, which I've always found attractive. I'm not someone who likes to envision life more than two or three years ahead at a time; if I imagine establishing myself, in a career or a relationship, I feel dead inside, the way a professor with tenure at some small college must feel when she realizes she has shackled herself to an institution, to a place, a routine, for decades of sameness.

I often remind myself that J. has been shaken by his illness, traumatized, even, and I am hoping that once he gets stronger, he'll become more like his former, irreverent self, that guy who spent long afternoons in the café. Before I got to know him, I'd refill his cup for free when I wanted to see what he was doing, what he was writing on those music sheets that had been photocopied too many times; the lines of each staff were barely visible, and his cramped handwriting illegible. Sometimes he held the pen in his nicotine-stained fingers as if it was a cigarette.

Smoking is terrible for Crohn's patients, but for now, I have stopped trying to get J. to quit. I used to leave messages for him on the kitchen counter when I went to work:

"Please quit cigarettes. —Sincerely, Your scratchy esophagus."

"Stop, you're killing me!—Your sad, sad heart."

"Cough-cough-cough-stop it! Cough-cough. —Your (cough) blackened lungs."

"Ouch! Cut it out, would ya?—Your colicky colon."

He did laugh at these notes, to his credit.

Otto & Shelley Go Shopping

Otto and Shelley go out to buy supplies before J.'s scheduled arrival. Otto failed the driving test last year and lost his licence; since then Shelley, afraid of the highway, drives their BMW on the back roads to the city for strudel, sauerkraut, sliced salami, and schnitzel from the specialty store. It's run by people from Pakistan, she thinks, or from some other place with a "stan" in it—who knows? The maps change every day! One day maybe even the towns we're from will disappear or get new names, Otto *says. It's happened before.*

Shelley and Otto have had to drive to get their favourite foods for a few years now. The deli on Main Street couldn't cover the rent anymore and closed, because the tourists don't come here for European foods. The Americans, the Koreans, the Japanese: they come for homemade ice cream, for a taste of the past, for taking selfies in front of old-fashioned storefronts that sell keychains and T-shirts with Canadian flags on them. How they've degraded this town!

Back in their driveway, Otto struggles with his seatbelt. He doesn't notice that Shelley is already out of the car, opening the trunk. She lifts out the grocery bags, carries two in each hand. It hasn't started to rain, but it will, because Shelley's fingers have been aching since dawn. The bags are heavy, and the plastic cuts into her flesh. Otto has managed to put only one foot down on the driveway by the time Shelley appears on his side of the car.

"Where the hell did you go? You always disappear on me!"

"What you are talking about, Otto? I'm right here." He is angry at his body, she knows, not at her; it is something that comes from a long marriage, this knowing. She offers her left arm to her husband for leverage, her elbow jutted and aimed at his ear. Otto rises.

I wonder if I should wake J. up now, just for his company.

Earlier today, before J. fell asleep beside me in the car, a transport truck full of pigs passed us on the left, and as soon as I saw beige-pink flesh pressing through the holes in its metal sides, I turned my head away.

"Hey!" J. said, grabbing the steering wheel. "Eyes on the road!" I slowed down, letting the truck get far enough ahead of us that I couldn't see the animals anymore. "We're carnivores, Sam," J. said. "It's an ugly fact of life."

"People eating meat doesn't bother me," I told him. "It's how they go about getting that meat. How the animals are treated. There's no reason pigs should be put into a loud, diesel-burning truck like that and subjected to high speeds and potholes and fumes and heat—in this heat, J.! My god! And they have to struggle to stay upright all the way to the slaughterhouse. Some get their legs broken on the way there. Can you *imagine* the fear? The terror they are feeling, flying down the highway like that?"

"I can *now*, thank you very much."

We must be getting close. Blue-and-white provincial road signs have started to appear, drawing attention to local attractions: vineyard tours, summer theatre, military forts, waterfalls. Everyone says Upton Bay itself is stunning; it's been voted the prettiest place to live in Canada more than once. But I've also noticed odd billboards popping up along the expressway: Kevin's Taxidermy—"keeping memories alive for twenty-five years"; Next Exit: Tender Fruit Association; Visit Evil Maple Estate Wines. I want to remember each one so I can tell J. about them later. He'll probably make up a story for each. He is good at impressions; he'll use a Dracula voice, I bet, for the taxidermy business, maybe an effeminate guy for the association, or a homophobic mafia character for the vintner. J. once made a few commercials in Toronto, after a scout in a pub where J. was playing talked to him between sets and got him signed; but J. drank too much to get to auditions on time, or keep to a shooting schedule. "Unreliably handsome" was the phrase J. used about himself when he told me about those days.

The radio in this fifteen-year-old VW has never worked. It might come on when I slam the driver's door, but it will turn off again at the first pothole or bump, or for no reason at all. The tape deck broke before the car became mine, too. While J. sleeps I try to find something on the radio but can't pull in a station.

After nearly two hours in the car, I am glad to see the turn-off just ahead, the sign announcing we are within town limits:

> You are entering
> UPTON BAY
> Population: 11,547

The road in the next stretch is flat, flanked by fields with hundreds of flags nailed to posts that stand in straight rows. Small grape vines are planted beside them. The flags must be some sort of deterrent for birds, I think.[2]

I jump every time I hear the sound of loud gunshots, which go off every few minutes as we pass acres of vineyards lining the old, two-lane road. Are rifles being fired at the fort, I wonder, to impress tourists?[3]

J. sleeps through every blast.

Another turn, and we land in a traffic jam. Way out here? Has there been an accident?[4]

We finally start moving, only to slow down again as cars pull over to buy from competing fruit stands set up in quickly assembled shelters. Farmers must come from miles away to sell the apples, peaches, and pears they've grown in

---

2 Sam is wrong: the flags are for species identification, so that workers don't harvest the wrong type of grape at the wrong time. Various colours are used to differentiate between plant types, because so many of the workers can't read English.

3 No. The noise is made by cannon recordings that scare birds away from the grapes.

4 Someone wants to turn left into a farmer's market and can't get a break, that's all. She'll get used to this pattern.

their orchards, since only grapes seem to be grown locally.

I notice two men passing my barely-moving car on bicycles—rusty, dented ten-speeds that glide along the unpaved shoulder of the two-way road to town—moving faster than the long, metal snake we've become part of. We soon catch up and pass them, but not for long; as they go past us for the second time, I see both cyclists are wearing woolen caps, though the temperature is eighty-five in the shade. The older man is in baggy jeans, a long-sleeved cotton undershirt beneath his buttoned plaid shirt; the younger, behind him, is in a sleeveless T-shirt and cut-offs, and gray gravel dust spun from their wheels coats his smooth, muscled calves.

Crime is on the rise

Meanwhile, in Upton Bay, there has been another break-in. 'Home invasion' is the preferred term.

It's an attack on our way of life! On civilization itself!

The Olivers, Debbie and Jerry, had been out for a late lunch at the golf club by the lake. She'd ordered a Caesar salad, but the romaine was limp, so she sent it back and accepted crab cakes on the house, in apology, instead. Jerry had the steak, medium rare, as usual. They returned home to find the back door wide open, sideboards emptied of silverware, bureau drawers in the main-floor master turned upside down on the Persian rug that had belonged to Debbie's grandmother. Rings, bracelets, and necklaces—passed down for generations—gone.

Debbie is sobbing and sobbing and sobbing, saliva and mucus in full flow. Jerry puts a box of Kleenex on the kitchen table in front of her. "At least they didn't burn the house down," he says, tearing off a sheet of paper towel; he wraps it around the telephone receiver, in case there are prints on it, before dialing the police. "We still have a roof over our heads."

An hour later, a cruiser pulls into Rose Carswell's driveway, next door to the Olivers, because there is nowhere else to park. A small group is gathered on the sidewalk in front of the Olivers' house: the Desmonds—Janet and Steve—are there, and old Frank Johnston, and Joan Palmer, too. Larry is away on business, Joan says, but she always says that when he is nursing the worst of his hangovers. Two officers approach and address Joan. She seems to be the one in charge.

"Did you happen to see or hear anything unusual, ma'am?"

"No," Joan says, "but everyone has suspicions."

A band of brazen gypsies. The Desmonds' wayward son. Migrants from the vineyards.

Illegal immigrants slipping across the border.

People who don't belong here.

"Unless we have witnesses, there's not much we can do. These guys are long gone by now and they won't sell the goods here. There's a network they'll use."

Picking locks on back doors! In the middle of the day!

Jerry is told to contact his insurance company. The second policeman offers his card. "Call me if you or your neighbours remember anything."

J. startles awake when the car approaches Main Street. It's as if he can smell his blood relations close by. He sits up too suddenly, grabs his abdomen. "Jesus! Fucking! Christ!"

I gently brake to a stop. There is nowhere to pull over, since cars are parked at the curb all the way down the street. Cars behind us start honking within seconds, so I pull into a flagstone driveway to let them pass.

"Sorry," J. says, lying back again, panting with pain. He rubs his side with his hand, using circular motions.

The hood of the VW is pointed at a restored brick Colonial, set well back from the street. Fluted white columns flank either side of a porticoed front door, painted red. An oversized, overstuffed blue recycling bin is on the grass next to my side of the car, filled with empty wine and liquor bottles.[5]

"Do you want another couple of pain pills? There's some water left in my bottle. Here. Sit up a little, or you'll choke."

J. pulls himself up to a forty-five-degree angle using the emergency handbrake for leverage and takes the thick tablets from my palm. He sips from the bottle and swallows them, then sticks his tongue out.

"Yuck. You could make tea with that water, it's so warm." He peers over the dash and looks ahead. He doesn't need to read the brass heritage plaque (FIELD HOUSE, ca. 1820) by the front door of the home to get his bearings.

"Pop's place is just a couple of blocks from here. Left at the stop sign. Sam?"

"What?"

"I wouldn't come here for just *anyone*, you know."

I am instantly irritated. J. has been making statements like this almost every day, pressing his feelings for me, *on* me. He is trying too hard. His stay with me is supposed to be temporary. And I'll only do his laundry at the Wash 'n' Dry around the corner for so long.

But he *is* doing me a favour right now, I have to give him that.

---

[5] The bins will multiply like rabbits after dark tonight, when the more discreet residents position their offerings for pick up in the morning.

Sam and J.'s arrival

Shelley hears a car door slam at the front of the house. She wipes her hands on an apron, heavy with hardened flour, and scoots down the hall, the heel-flattened back of her old felt slippers flapping. "He's here!" she yells as she passes the living room. But Otto's hearing aids are not in his ears. He has fallen asleep in his lounger chair, the Town Crier *spread across his lap.*

"God, that awful chair," Shelley mutters to herself. "Big enough for a bed, and he uses it like one."

Fiddling with the deadbolt and knob, Shelley leaves wet-floured fingerprints that will soon harden to glue.[6] Shelley flings the door open and stands at the threshold, frozen, watching J.'s shoes slowly emerge under the open passenger door of an old car that should not, by the looks of it, be on the road. At least it's German, she thinks—Otto might appreciate that. J.'s soles touch ground just as the back of a blond head comes into view in the window of the open door; she is bent forward, offering J. the X she's made of her forearms, and J. locks his grip around the thumb of each hand. Then she leans back, pulling J. up toward her, and he rises to a standing position. She turns and J. puts his left arm around her shoulders. Her right foot reaches behind her, kicking the door shut.

When Shelley steps forward and greets them, the two heads tip up, like synchronized swimmers on cue, to look at her.

The woman, who must be Shelley, cups her face in her hands. "Oh, J.! What has happened to you? You look terrible!"

---

[6] They will stay there until Otto's daughter comes to prepare the house for sale.

I half smile, but notice that J.'s jaw is tense.

"Shell," he says, "I'm fine. It's a bad flu this year, that's all."

I had asked J. to warn Shelley about the change in him since they'd last seen him, five years ago, but J. said it was better not to, that Shelley would only exaggerate and upset Otto for nothing. He had no intention of telling them anything about his hospitalization or diagnosis.

"Listen," says J., stopping and touching Shelley's shoulder. "I want you to meet Samara."

Shelley turns and pecks me on both cheeks, as Europeans do.

"Thank you for bringing him here, Miss—"

"It's Sam. Samara Johansen."

"Johansen? You're Swedish, then."

"Close," I say. "My mother's Norwegian."

"Oh, I see," Shelley says, but I see an edge in her expression that I recognize: the same set to the mouth, that slight downturn of the lips that Besta donned whenever she was pretending kindness.

Shelley turns back to J. "Otto will be so excited to see you in the flesh, J.! Please, come in, come in. You too, Miss—"

"Just call me Sam."

Inside, J. finds Otto sleeping in the living room, and he whispers to Shelley that he needs to lie down, too. Shelley leads him to the large, main-floor guest room and closes the door. To me, she says, "Come," and we head to the kitchen. I notice grab bars are installed all the way down the long hallway that runs from the front to the back of the house.

"So, Miss—I mean, Sam. Sit, sit down, Sam, while I peel potatoes." She offers me a cold bottle of Löwenbräu, cap off, which I accept; it was a long, hot drive.

"Wait, wait—I've got glasses! We're not peasants here!"

Shelley sits next to me at the table and pours my beer into a tall crystal glass. "These are from John," she says, "J.'s father. He used to bring us things from his business trips, I don't know why. We needed nothing. These glasses are heavy for us old people to lift to our faces!"

I smile, but Shelley looks serious.

"I don't know what J. has told you," she says, "but once upon a time I was called the *younger* woman. Compared to Otto. But he wasn't an old man then, either."

What is she is trying to persuade me of, I wonder. That Otto was a catch, back in the day?

"We had our fun," she adds, winking. "But after a while, he'd land in bed like a sack of flour, already asleep. Anyway, after you turn sixty, the age difference doesn't really matter anymore. Now I just want to go to sleep, too!"

Shelley has spread pages of a newspaper across the table and places a colander of rinsed russets in front of her. She chooses one with her left hand and pushes the peeler against it with her right, moving it away from her body with deep, hard strokes, as if she is scything a field. Clear brown water spatters the paper, all around the growing pile of skins, some with chunks of yellow flesh attached.[7]

"Are you going to tell me what's going on with J.? He looks like death."

I take another sip of beer. "He was sick for a while," I say. "Don't worry, everything is okay now. He's doing well."

"He doesn't *look* well."

"So, what kind of business trips did John take?" I know it is obvious that I'm trying to change the subject, but I really do wonder what John is like. "J. hasn't told me much about his dad, other than he runs restaurants in town."

---

7   Sam will end up piling an extra helping of potatoes on her plate, next to the pork, at dinner; J. forgot to tell Shelley that Sam is a vegetarian.

"That's right. Before, though, John worked with Otto in the business."

"Upholstery, right? In Kitchener?"

"No no no, Otto and his *first* wife ran that business. They moved to Upton when they closed the shop, and Otto also sold some land he'd bought in the area when the kids were little. *Then* he started in the hotel business. The hotels here were bad, then—like biker bars, really. Grete wanted nothing to do with them, but she had a big-shot uncle still living in Munich, and he took Otto on a tour of the grand hotels of Europe. To show him the standards, you know, before he got set up. He loaned them money at first. Otto bought two buildings and renovated and paid back the loan, all in about three years."

"That's impressive."

"Very impressive. Otto was a very smart businessman. Then John came on, when he decided he didn't want to practice law in Toronto anymore and moved here with his wife and J.J.; Otto made him some kind of manager. But after Otto retired, John ran out of money."

"I would think the hotel business would be quite lucrative here, based on the prices I saw on websites."

"Well, it *was*, when *Otto* ran things. But… well, to be fair, the competition got worse. It's the Chinese, mostly, that's what John thinks. They've taken over so much here—the hotels, the restaurants, the shops. This Hong Kong lady bought one hotel, then another, and she modernized them. Wiped away the charm, the history of the buildings—that's what she *really* did. She got away with it, somehow, despite the building heritage rules. Money can buy you anything, right? She probably bribed the councillors, it wouldn't surprise me. And John started to lose bookings. More money from Otto, more all the time, directly down the drain. Before they went bankrupt, Otto sold—but not to the Chinese lady, I'll tell you that. I think it was a small

Toronto chain, I don't know… they paid Otto well enough. Then he bought two small diners, one downtown, one on the outskirts. For John to run."

"Sounds like John is one lucky guy, with Otto as his father."

"Well, they were both run down. Old-time places, with all-day scrambled eggs and not much else, but these tourists, I tell you, they want fancy-schmancy, not mom-and-pop food, John said. So, Otto gave him money to renovate, to change the menu. *Then* they started to do better, so John was right for once. You should go see them with J. tomorrow."

I know that J. will not go near either of his father's establishments, but I have no qualms about going myself. Perhaps I'll interview customers and staff, compile neutral information about "where to eat" for my article. J. doesn't have to know every detail about my day.

Shelley tells me about the bicycle business that the nephew of a friend opened recently. "You might get a free rental, if you offer to mention them in your article."

I think of the two men I saw biking, on our way into town; the models they rode were like the ten-speed I had in high school, except theirs had partial, rusted chain guards and no fenders. "If their fleet is as beat up as the bikes I saw people riding on the highway today, I'd rather walk."

"Oh, you must mean the migrants. Those men who come from Mexico and Jamaica and wherever, to work as labourers in the vineyards. They get loaner wheels as part of the package. They ride in from the orchards to get groceries."

"All those miles along the highway, on a bike?"

"It's free transportation!" Shelley says, her hands in the air as if to say, *What do you expect?* "Anyway," she continues, "I won't drive on the highway, and no bus or train service comes here. I'd love to go to the outlet mall they built on the expressway. Maybe the two of us could go on a girls' outing, while you're here? Even when Otto could drive, he was always too stingy to take me."

I finish my beer and suggest I should take my bag to our room, down the hall, where J. had already gone to lie down.

"Please, we would like you to have the guest room, upstairs."

"But J. would prefer the main floor, it's just easier for him."

"Fine, fine. But we are old-fashioned people, I'm afraid. So you will be upstairs, if you don't mind…"

At dinner, J. asks Otto about a piece of art he remembers from his childhood.

"Where's that painting I always liked? The small watercolour you used to have on the wall—with tall houses scrunched together on a hill, in colours like ochre and army green and dark purple. Remember? You could see the sketch lines under the paint."

Otto drops his fork and it bounces from his plate to the tiled kitchen floor, spraying grease and clattering everyone to silence. Shelley goes to get a new one, and Otto squints at his food as if he might find the answer to J.'s question in the mashed potatoes, roast pork, or sauerkraut.

"It's here somewhere," he says, bending to wipe up the drops of fat with his paper napkin. "Shelley changes things around sometimes. Right, Shell?"

"I don't know what happened to it either, J." Shelley smiles and sits down again. "But it came from Grete's family. Maybe she did something with it, who knows. Or your mother, J. Maybe she took it."

Otto has finished eating and tries to rise from the table, but his knee gives out and he falls back in his chair, hard.

"J., help him, please?" Shelley says. "He needs to get to his big chair. They call it an 'easy' chair," she says to me, "but it's not so easy on the eyes."

I know she wants to keep talking to me about how ugly the chair is, but I also know that J. can't help, so I stand up and support Otto's elbow with my hand. Otto is much older than I expected him to be, and I wonder how J. feels about seeing his grandfather's decline. It must seem drastic; he hasn't watched it happen gradually over the years, which would make it easier to get used to. And Otto's memory must be going, too, if he can't place a painting that had been hanging in his house for decades. We finally reach the living room, Otto and I, and he collapses into his chair.

J. makes his own slow way into the room and sits on the sofa next to Otto.

I go back to the kitchen, but Shelley won't let me start on the dishes.

"No. You are a guest in our home. No way you're doing housework. Go and relax with those two."

J. knows I would rather log onto the internet with my laptop than hang out with him and his grandfather. When he tells Otto that I have to work, I feel something like tenderness toward J.

An hour later, feeling guilty for leaving him with Otto, I come downstairs to find J. has already gone to bed. From the door to the living room, I watch as Shelley slides pills through Otto's open mouth onto his tongue and inserts a straw. Her face is plump and smooth, but her arms give away her age: the skin has that cross-hatched, dried-out, crepe-like quality, and the fat under her upper arm wobbles while she waits for Otto to respond. Otto clamps his lips around the plastic tube and sucks, then swallows twice before turning his head away.

I go back upstairs to prepare for my workday tomorrow.

After everyone else has gone to bed and the house is quiet, I can't sleep, so I wander back down into the living room. I lift the *Town Crier* from the floor where it slid off Otto's lap. Much of the paper is filled with advertising: local restaurants (which ones belong to J.'s dad, I wonder?), clothing boutiques, corny musicals and play productions. "Our Town" is playing in one of the theatres, and tickets are apparently still available starting at $200. Underneath the photo of the program is a boxed notice that Rob Phillips, the Conservative MP for the riding, will be making a funding announcement from his local office regarding the arts next week. I cringe at the wide, smiling face of Mr. Phillips, because I've read about him tabling a bill to institute measures that would legalize the withholding of evidence from Canadians held in prison on a security certificate. I wonder why that word, "measures," is used for legal documents that take away people's rights?

The Letters to the Editor section includes one submission about the lack of parking in town ("residents can't even find a spot in the Canada Post lot, because tourists leave their cars there for hours!") and another long entry that runs over to the next page:

NOT IN MY TOWN

Re: building on waterfront

The monstrosity under construction on Front Street next to the golf course is not only completely out of character with the historic architecture of our town, but it blocks the view from the Williams's heritage home situated across the street, which has been there for over two hundred years. Andrew

Williams must be rolling over in his grave! The owners, who (though Jewish) made their fortune selling Christmas ornaments year-round, clearly do not care about our traditions, but what has happened to the values of our trusted councillors on the Heritage and Construction Committee? They are the ones who are allowing this build to proceed. We'd like answers, please.

  Beryl and Carol Crawford

I can picture the pair of them, seated side by side at a walnut dining table that had been a wedding gift to their parents from Grandmother Crawford; one sister—the older one, who has grown out the short perm her sibling still sports, and piles her thinning hair on top of her head—is reading their letter aloud from the *Crier*. The younger listens, face glistening with pride.[8]

Then I read another letter, from a realtor in the area:

TOO FAR, TOO FAST

Re: progress is not as important as the environment.

This town is at a tipping point, on a collision course between its past and its future. We've grown this

---

8   Sam is correct about how she envisions the Crawford sisters: spinsters in white blouses and stretchy black pants, their thick waists hidden by rooster-patterned aprons. They bake apple, cherry, and peach pies for the United Church's seasonal sales each summer to raise funds for repairs to the rectory. They volunteer at the hospital and the library. "We are busier now than when we were teaching!" they assure past students, who come back home for Christmas and summer holidays and who turn around on the sidewalk if they see the sisters first.

place over two hundred years of history. We've experienced a few spurts now and then, but in the last ten years there has been way too much development, way too fast. If we keep going for another decade at this pace, we're going to ruin our heritage. That's what it's starting to feel like, with outside developers trying to influence council to tweak bylaws and bypass the provincial heritage status of certain acreage.

Tim Barton, Registered Real Estate Broker

Eventually I fall asleep in the upstairs guest room, with questions these letters prompted floating through my mind: *Who is allowed in? Who can stay? And who is chased away?*

MONDAY

I'm not feeling well this morning. My neck is tight and my gut hurts, and when I walk down the hall to the bathroom, I am slightly off balance. My ears are buzzing. It's likely from a lack of sleep, and from the humid weather. It could be the start of another migraine, this general lack of wellbeing. I will probably need to take naproxen today, as a preventive, but I hope I can forego the Gravol, which makes me foggy-headed.

I pull on some jeans and a T-shirt. I'll have to ask Shelley about who her neighbours are, to get some background information about who lives in this town other than old, white, antisemitism people with parking concerns. I have a lot to learn before I'll be able to write a word about the appeal of Upton Bay to tourists.

Shelley is in the kitchen making coffee. Both Otto and J. are sleeping in.

"Morning," I say, reaching for the mug Shelley holds out to me. The coffee wakes me up but makes my stomach churn.

"Sam," Shelley says. "That's such a masculine name for a pretty girl like you."

I smile a little, pouring more cream into my cup. Shelley holds her face very steady, watching me.

"I know it is short for Samara. But that's not Norwegian, is it?"

"It's Russian, actually. Samara was the name of my grandmother's best friend, whose family was Jewish. They left Russia for Norway because of the pogroms."

"Oh, my god. I didn't even know there *were* Jews in Norway!" Again, with that forced smile.

"So, Shelley," I venture, "I'll be starting my research today. I need to find out what people like about this place. I need to talk to tourists, but I also want to talk with residents, like you and Otto. I know you met him at his hotel. But how did Otto end up in Upton? What drew him here?"

"He came here to retire because it's beautiful, and because good people live here."

"Good people?"

"Doctors, dentists, professors—you know, good classes of people."

"Are you from Upton?"

"No, I'm from Kitchener. My family is still there. I could have met Otto there, but life is funny like that, isn't it? Anyway, in Kitchener they have so many people with drug problems now, and the homeless are always hanging around downtown. I'm glad I moved away."

"And Otto came here because… ?"

"Didn't J. tell you? Well, maybe he doesn't remember. Oh—of course not, what am I thinking! It's John who would know. J. wasn't even—what's the expression? A glint of his father's smile?"

"In his father's eye," I say. "Otto must have made some smart investments, to afford his life in Upton."

"Oh, Otto is a smart man, you know. He bought fruit farms here, cheap, when he still lived in Kitchener. Kitchener was called Berlin before, because so many German people came to live there in the 1800s, including my family. I can trace my ancestors to pre-Napoleonic times! My parents' great-grandparents immigrated from Westphalia in the 1830s. There is all this information you can get now on the internet, did you know? The government has put census forms online, going way back. For instance, I know what my great-great-grandfather grew on his land in 1851. I have a file somewhere with information about how much land he had when he came here, and what crops he grew.[9] My great-grandfather became a printer. He published a German-language newspaper. So in one generation, the Schmidts stopped living off the land and started living off the written word. Imagine that!"

"That's interesting," I say, though it isn't what I asked her. "So, Otto—"

"Oh, Kitchener was a very different place by the time Otto arrived in the fifties. The 1950s, that is. He got off the boat a hundred years after my family did. And Upton has changed a lot in all the time we've both lived here, too, of course."

"How do you mean?"

"Oh. I shouldn't say it, but the tour buses, they bring all these people without manners. Who knows where they come from. And some of the neighbours, you know? They don't come from such good families, maybe. Joan Palmer,

---

9 From Shelley's files:

```
1851 AGRICULTURAL CENSUS—CANADA WEST, LAMBTON
   COUNTY ENUMERATION DISTRICT NO. SEVEN
NAME OF OCCUPIER             ACRES OF LAND
                   Conc.  Held Crops Pasture Orch Wood
Dirk Schmidt         1     200   55*                145
WHEAT*       BARLEY*       RYE*
Acres Bsh.   Acres Bsh.    Acres  Bsh.
 18    360    18    360     18    360
```

she lives across the street—" Shelley points to the window "—she and her husband, they drink too much. Always trouble happening, between those two."

Shelley clearly wants to tell me stories about the Palmers, but not the kind of stories I'm looking for. I glance at the clock and mumble something about getting properly dressed, then go back upstairs to rest my head, taking my coffee with me.

Joan Palmer is up to something

Summers are always the worst.

The tourists, of course, but not only that.

Not only the bus loads of Japanese and Chinese who keep themselves in line formation on their guided walking tours through town, stopping to pose in front of certified, historically accurate homes as if they are wandering through a movie set for a film about Empire Loyalists.

Not only the overweight Americans who drive their chubby children across the border in SUVs on weekends and walk very slowly, three and four across, on the wide, main-street sidewalks, window shopping at the high-priced trinket-laden shops and eating baseball-sized scoops of ice cream as they shuffle along to find hamburgers with maple syrup fixings, to tide them over until supper.

Not only the migrants who appear out of nowhere on bikes and line up at the post office to wire money, or at the grocery store to buy pop and potato chips.

Not the other dark ones, either—those who come in second-hand cars without air conditioning, with patches of body-fill paste painted in shades that don't disguise the repair; they picnic on front lawns when the nearby public park gets too crowded for one more family to plant its coolers on the crest of the small rise by the rocky waterfront.

None of that helps, of course, but it's not this deluge that scores Joan's nerves at the cusp of summer every year. It's Larry.

Larry at the pool parties, the patio dinner parties, the outdoor brunches; Larry, drinking round after round of gin and tonic before moving to straight vodka over ice. Summer invitations make Larry's drinking socially acceptable and his violence at home a seasonal hazard.

On a cool June night, two years ago, after Larry singed her abdomen with a fire brand, Joan found out that the overgrown path connecting the driveway to a side door was too narrow for paramedics to get their equipment through. They'd always parked the ambulance in front and walked up the wide, flagstone walkway before, but that night there were vehicles with plates from New York, Michigan, and Quebec parked end-to-end in front of the house, blocking the path to the front door. So they'd had to take Joan out between them in a carry chair, instead, with her face in full view.

Worse, while Joan was housebound as she recovered, the occupants of another car blocking the walkway picked up the flower urns that had graced the start of her flagstone path and put them in their trunk, driving off with them.

Once well enough, Joan petitioned the town to have this prime spot clearly marked as off-limits for parked cars. Council eventually agreed to the request—the whole town knew what Larry was like, that ambulance calls were fairly regular—but the Works Department hadn't refreshed the words NO PARKING, painted across diagonal ochre lines on the asphalt, since.

Now Joan is tired of fending off drivers who can't see the faded markings, tired of putting down those neon orange cones she'd taken from a construction site on the edge of town last week. Even that had been a complete waste of time: they'd disappeared within hours! The hardware store couldn't keep them in stock, *apparently; Ronald, the manager, told Joan that store owners used cones to keep delivery pathways on Main Street clear, but tourists just run them down or pick them up and put them in their car, then take the parking spot as if it were their due. When Ronald asked the police to retrieve a set he'd seen tossed into a vehicle's trunk, he was lectured on unlawful search and seizure and human rights. "Do you believe that?" he said to Joan. "We live here and pay taxes! What about our rights?"*

Joan even spoke to John Sommerfeld about it a couple of years ago. He was a new town councillor then, and he had always been friendly toward her, unlike his father, Otto.

John ran for mayor last year; he lost, despite his white-toothed smile and easy saunter along the sidewalks, glossy brochures in hand. When he was out campaigning one afternoon, he told Joan—he'd spotted her sitting alone, at the patio bar of the bayside hotel his father used to own—that for him, the prize of winning would be getting an office in the former courthouse on Main Street, where council did its business. The courthouse was perfect for him because he'd always envisioned himself, in fact, as a man of the law. Joan laughed out loud at that, picturing John in a sheriff's uniform—the kind little boys wear when they go out trick or treating, with the plastic guns, the hat, the holster, and a star-shaped badge pinned to a vest. Then she said she thought he <u>was</u> a man of the law already, wasn't he? As a lawyer?

Then John told Joan a secret: when he was twenty-two, after earning a business diploma in Toronto, he told his parents he'd been admitted to law school in Ottawa. Otto had deposited money to his account for tuition and rent for over three years. Then his wife supported them on her salary working at Eaton's for a couple of years.

"I told Pop I was homesick. I said, 'Pop, I want to live here, where you are, and you know there's no room for another lawyer in this town.' That's all it took. He's a softie inside. He made

me his business partner, and he was so happy!" John laughed hard, slapped both hands on his thighs. "He said, 'You're the only one I can rely on, son.'"

When Joan smiled a little, John said, "But you know, I _am_," he insisted. "My sister never shows her face. I'm still here, am I not?"

"Yes, yes you are. And so am I, which is a problem if Larry gets home before I do. Thanks for the company and the Bloody Caesar, young man. Good luck." She held out her hand, wrinkly and soft, and John shook it.

"Good night." John stood and watched Joan take her leave, one slow, high-heeled step at a time, until she disappeared behind a hedge along the sidewalk. *She's too old for those shoes*, he thought, *especially if she's going to keep drinking like that.*

John stayed at the bar, campaigning into the night. The next morning, he used coffee to swallow down the aspirin he should have taken with glasses of water the night before. John had the vague sense he'd told Joan about something that he shouldn't have. *What did I tell that old slut?* he wondered. (The question bothered him for a few days, but he hasn't thought of it since.) He felt a stiffening of his lungs, a shortening of his breath, and a familiar cool, prickling sensation moving out from his core and across the surface of his arms and legs, his face tingling. Hyperventilation—John's curse when he was small and afraid to go to school, where an older boy there would pinch him, punch him, make him cry. His mother used to call his reaction *der zingels. He was too sensitive for a boy*, Grete would say to Otto, her voice carrying through the house at night. She was always so critical, and she was much harder to fool than his father was.

It is very early in the morning when Joan picks up the phone and dials her next-door-neighbour's number. She has new a plan that is sure to deter tourist parking.

"Rose," Joan says, "come over, will you? I need you to help me with something." Joan Palmer wears a slight British accent, though she is really from a small town in the United States.

Behind her back, Joan calls Rose the Dummy or D.O.M., for Dull Old Maid. She doesn't know that Rose had been married once, a long time ago. She doesn't even remember Rose's last name.

Wearing a coffee-splashed eyelet housecoat with faintly yellowed armpits, Rose arrives at the end of the driveway just as Joan steps outside. Joan walks toward her, a can of yellow spray paint in hand. It is going to be a humid day, but she hopes it won't rain until later in the afternoon.

Joan points to a spot about ten feet away from where the two women are standing. "Lie down there."

"Lie down?"

"That's right. On your back."

Rose starts to lower herself, knees first, onto the narrow grass boulevard.

"For god's sake," Joan shouts, "not there! On the pavement!" She steps quickly off the curb into the empty space between two parked cars. "Here!" Rose does as she is told. She always does, when it comes to Joan.

Joan positions Rose's right arm in a ninety-degree angle at the elbow, palm facing up. Then she makes a triangle of Rose's legs, right heel to left knee, yanking the hem of her robe to cover her lace-trimmed bloomers. Jesus, thinks Joan, can you not wear pyjama bottoms like everyone else your age? Joan pauses, hands on hips, and studies Rose's face, as if she were studying a model sitting for her portrait.

"Turn your head to the right, would you? There. Good. Now close your eyes."

Joan holds the can upside down and shakes it back and forth, listening to the clacking sound made by little metal *balls inside. She depresses the nozzle once and releases it very quickly, testing the pressure of the spray. The odour is strong, and Rose lifts her head and opens her mouth, about to protest. "Keep still, Rose," Joan says as she bends forward. As she sprays, she takes a slow walk around Rose, and a three-inch-wide band of paint bleeds out from the contours of her neighbour's body.*

I can hear everything in this house from my perch upstairs. The walls are very thin, as if wallpaper had been pasted directly onto the lathe strips.

J. has just risen.

"Well, hello!" Otto says to J. from his living room chair. "Are you sure you should be up so early?"

"No, I'm not sure at all!" J. laughs. "Let me grab a coffee, Pop."

Shelley doesn't say anything to J., so she must not be in the kitchen.

"So, J.," Otto says when J. is back. "I think we should have a talk."

"No Pop, not if it's about my dad."

"No no no, *nein*, this is about you. You and the girl."

"Her name is Sam. And she's not a girl, she's thirty."

"Thirty! Older than you! What's her family background?"

"Her mother was born in Norway but grew up in Sudbury. She raised Sam by herself."

"A single mother?"

"So what? My parents had me and then broke up, and my mother became a complete alcoholic who kicked me out of the house. Not to mention my father, who isn't exactly a paragon of virtue, is he?"

"At least you know who your parents were. You can trace your lineage."

"Oh, don't tell me. You think I should see only German girls or something, to keep our bloodlines pure?"

"Stop!" shouts Otto. He must have held his hand up in the air when he said that, because then J. says, "Jesus, Pop! What's that supposed to be, a salute? *Heil!*"

"That's enough, J.! Your father said you are difficult, that you don't listen, but I defended you. Maybe I was wrong to do that."

The TV comes on and all I can hear after that is a news channel from Buffalo.

J. comes in just as I'm putting a notebook in my tote bag.

"Hey—you made it up the stairs! I'm just about to leave."

J. picks up the tourism brochure that I'd left lying on the bed, and reads from it:

> "The Heritage District in Upton Bay is made for walking, with its boutique shops, cast-iron planters bursting with flowers, and horse-drawn carriages transporting riders to another time and place."

"What a bullshit town this is," he says. Then he asks me if I'm comfortable here.

"Well, the air is stifling, but the bed's okay."

"No, I mean, here," he says, gesturing with his arms, "around my grandfather."

"He doesn't seem to like me, does he? He's hardly looked at me."

"I know. Downstairs, he just asked me what your background is. And then he got angry at me when I pressed him about why it matters."

"Don't worry about it. He can ask me if he likes, I'll tell him. And I'll ask him all about his background, too. There—a topic for conversation at dinner tonight."

"I wouldn't bother if I were you. He's never told me anything. When I was about twelve, my mother drove me back here to interview my grandparents about their lives before they came to Canada, for a school project, and all they would say was, 'That was a difficult time for everybody. We live here now. We are Canadians, like you.' Even my father couldn't tell me anything. I had to make up stories about their lives, just so I wouldn't fail the assignment."

"Don't worry, I won't bring it up. He's letting us stay here, right? Just remember that. Don't let him get to you. Gotta go."

I step out the front door and inhale the fresh air. I feel as though I slept in a closet all night because the window sash in the room had been painted shut a long time ago and I couldn't open it. I look at the Victorian homes along the street, with their still, ancient willow and maple trees shading them. Where I grew up, greenery of any kind was scarce. When I moved to Toronto for university, I told new friends that living up north is like living on the moon: the deep shield that covers vast areas is so unyielding that nothing short of dynamite made it at all passable; even then, huge slabs of striated rock on either side of the roads made me feel as though I were barely escaping a gargantuan vice everywhere I went. I've never gotten past the idea that the land itself was trying to get rid of me.

The heat of the day is already building, and I can smell the exhaust of an idling bus wafting toward me from Main. Across the street, drivers looking for a parking place keep signalling and stopping, then immediately pulling away. When I cross the road, I can see why no one claims it: a life-sized outline of a body is painted on the pavement.

How strange; the town is hardly known for its high crime rate. Not a useful bit for my article, but nonetheless I take a picture of the yellow image, and decide it is too TV-perfect a shape to be real. Maybe it's part of the evening walking tour I've read about: there are these nighttime prowls that take groups tramping over haunted grounds, into storied old hotel pubs, looking for ghosts. I'll mention this odd entertainment in my piece; maybe I'll buy a ticket to see firsthand what the experience of shadow-seeking is like. J. won't want me to go, not after I've left him alone with Otto and Shelley all day.

Up on Main Street, I approach the streaming mid-day crowd and take pictures of the hordes in front of the boutiques. My photos won't be used, but they'll prompt me to write some of the copy. My own caption would read: "Though overcrowded with young families and their Hummer-sized baby carriages, slow-walking couples holding hands, and busloads of elderly theatre goers arriving in time for the matinee, the town draws people who enjoy wandering in and out of Upton's specialty shops—buying everything within reach, from thousand-dollar leather jackets to costume jewellery, from fudge and homemade pies to home décor from Provençal." All of which the editor would translate into this: "Lively and popular, Main Street offers something for everyone!"

I deke down a side street that is slightly less thick with sticky bodies and sit at a table for two that had opened up as I walked into the cafeteria-style café. The place is packed. The outdoor patio behind the building has umbrellas that match the cloths on tables and the pillows on chairs, arranged in small rows beneath the arching branches of old oak trees. The food is Italian; the smell of oregano, onion, and garlic makes me salivate, as does the menu's list of paninis and pastas and salads, with recommended local wines for each. I wonder about the history of the area's agriculture—what grew on the farms that used to be here, when the population lived off the land? Before the vineyards?

I order a glass of shiraz from Evil Maple Estates. What a name. I'll be going to that vineyard tomorrow, so I tell myself that research is in order. There is no drinking around J. these days; his doctors told him to abstain from alcohol completely and, so far, he has followed their advice. I take a sip of wine, my first in months, and I am surprised by how much I like the rich, peppery taste.

As I approach Main Street, I see that the afternoon theatre crowd is going in for drinks before the 2:00 p.m. show. There are two shows on, one in each of the venues in this building: *The Pyjama Game* and *Guys and Dolls*. I see several loud, laughing white women in groups of three or four, most sporting short, silver coiffures and wearing colourful sleeveless dresses, carrying loosely woven shawls or sweaters for the air conditioning. Couples in their sixties and seventies, also white, form an orderly line at the bar, the men in suit jackets that used to fit them twenty years ago but wouldn't close now if they tried to button them.

Once most ticket holders have filed into the lobby bar area, I approach the box office to collect playbills and brochures and to inquire if I might have a word with the manager. The employee tells me that only the Public Relations and Publicity officer is permitted to speak with the media, and *only* by appointment. I am looking for quick conversations, not official quotes, but okay, I think, and take the P.R. woman's card. Before I can say thank you, the box office clerk has turned away.

John goes to work

John is driving up Otto's street to town hall this morning when he sees Joan Palmer standing on her front lawn, very thin, hands on hips. She looks like she's been cut out of a photo from the sixties and pasted into the scene. Joan is wearing a pink cotton blouse with pale blue pants and those large round sunglasses of hers, though the sun is still rising behind her house. He's reminded of their tête à tête *the year before, when he tried to guess the facial expression behind her dark lenses as he talked on and on—about what, he still has no idea. And it bothers him again now.*

Instead of preparing his items for the next council meeting or reconciling the restaurants' receivables figures, John spends hours at his desk with only a pad and pencil, ranking and re-ranking what he calls his "professional concerns" or "PCs." He ponders possible replies to imagined questions for each of them, should anyone ask. Satisfied, he reviews his work, then tears off and crumples the pages he's used. He tosses them into the recycling box beside his desk before he leaves for lunch. [10] *The secretary is glad he is not in a talkative mood, for once, when he passes her desk. John merges into the sidewalk foot traffic and edges his way to the curb, where his BMW awaits. His car window is darkly tinted so he can't be seen, once inside, but everyone knows which car is his.*

He eats for free at one of his restaurants but tips the waitress very well. Before going back to work, John takes a walk, trying

---

10   The secretary will remember this detail later.

to decide what obscure line he should use this month to park the "premium percentage" (or PP) of net that he takes for himself. Accounting principles are such wonderful tools! he thinks; they give you so many lenses for looking at a set of numbers, before deciding which is best for your purposes. He turns down the last block of Linden Street, which leads to the picnic area that sits on a rise overlooking Lake Ontario. He avoids walking by his father's house, one block up; Otto often sits on the front porch in daylight hours, and John does not want to see him until the ledger issue is settled in his mind. Otto must mark it on his calendar, John thinks, since he's never forgotten to ask about the balance sheet on the date it is supposed to go to his accountant. The man has a memory like an elephant.

John looks up the street and sees a wine-coloured car parked in his father's driveway. A Golf, if he's not mistaken, but an old model. Must be Sandy, he thinks, the fellow Shelley's sister used to live with. He spends more time talking than working, John complains to his father whenever he finds Sandy at the house. "Relax," Otto always says, "he's like another son, helping me. You're too busy." Handrails on the wall, washers for the taps, eavestrough gutters cleared out in the fall. Sure, thinks John, charging you by the hour for conversations that go nowhere. And dragging that ugly recliner from his parents' basement into the living room, where Otto sits and sleeps and watches TV. No wonder Shelley is upset about that second-hand blob. Sandy said it was barely used; it had been delivered by Sears just before his father died. How much did Pop pay him for it, under the table?

John should review his father's chequing and savings accounts, now that he thinks about it.

I hadn't known what kind of money J.'s family had before I came to Upton Bay and saw for myself. We had both started out with little, me and J.—he'd moved out of his mother's small house at sixteen and his father never did pay child support. But J. had known wealth through Otto, I see that now, whereas I grew up playing with empty shampoo bottles for dolls. (That's the kind of detail my best friend, Fern, likes to hear about my past. She can't imagine not having had toys to play with, new clothes for every season, a bank account of her own since she was ten. The first time I saw her parents' house in an upscale Toronto neighbourhood, where Fern still lives, I couldn't imagine having grown up with so much of everything.)

In the window of Upton Realty Inc.—owned, I note, by that Letter-to-the-Editor writer, Tim Barton—there are photographs of several homes for sale. The prices are much higher here than in Toronto, which are high enough. I'm guessing it's not older people who are moving here to retire anymore; it must be young stockbroker types, with money to burn—money to invest in restorations of two-hundred-year-old mansions, in building wineries and microbreweries. There is a craft beer pub on the way into town, I noticed yesterday, and I've already walked by another on Main Street today. There are more wineries and breweries per capita in the area, the brochures say, than anywhere else in the province.

The sidewalks on Main are filled with tourists who seem to be sleepwalking as they slowly move from storefront to storefront, carrying large bags from clothing boutiques and smaller ones from artisanal cheese and chocolate shops, whose staff stuff colourful tissue paper on top of the purchases to make them look like presents.

On the way back to Otto's house, I wave at an old couple sitting on their front veranda, its white cotton porch curtains blowing like laundered sheets on the line from a sudden wind. They stare but don't wave back. A horse clip-clops by, pulling a just-married couple in the carriage behind it, and the porch people wave to them. I'm reminded of the video of the region's infamous serial killer and his accomplice, who'd taken a public horse-and-carriage nuptial tour here. Though they'd married long before anyone knew what they'd done, the video went viral after their arrests. If business had suffered from the bad publicity, you wouldn't know it now. People don't remember things for very long.

Otto is in the living room with J. when I get back. The TV volume is set as loud as the speakers in a movie theatre. I wave to J. from the hallway door and point to the ceiling, then mime the washing of my hair.

"You know," Otto says to J. after I am out of sight, "you see Blacks doing the news on all the stations now, and they're pretty good."

I hear J. say he needs to lie down and, as he is leaving the room, he greets Shelley on her way in to sit with Otto. I stand on the landing so I can hear what they say to each other.

"The girl barely speaks," Otto says. "She makes me nervous."

I know Shelley hasn't warmed to me either, but she surprises me. "She is smart and attractive. She talks to *me.*"

"J. doesn't look so good. His father would not be happy to see him like that. We should tell him."

"J. made me promise not to," says Shelley. "We're going to have fish tonight. Janet Desmond called this morning about a dinner they're having for the neighbours, to help us forget about the break ins, she says. She wants us to bring J. and Sam along, but we're not going to do *that*, not the way J. looks. Have you asked how long he will be staying with us, so I can plan the meals, Otto?"

Otto pretends he hasn't heard the question.

Then the phone rings, and Otto says, "Get that, will you?"

Enough, I think, and head to the shower.

The Desmonds host a party

Janet has a smooth face, lips the shape of Lucille Ball's, and bright blue eyes. Steve met her at Toronto General, the prettiest nursing student in her class. In the fifties, medical interns earned less than $300 a year, so Janet's salary supported them until Steve finished specializing in cardiology. Then she turned to gourmet cooking and mothering her two children. She had a reputation among the doctors and wives in their social set for throwing the most fabulous dinner parties, back in the day.

Tonight, Janet tells her guests that Shelley and Otto are not able to come. "There will be a lot of leftovers, so be prepared to eat more than your share tonight."

The string of robberies has brought the group together. Yesterday it was the Olivers, but tomorrow it could be the Sommerfelds, the Desmonds, the Palmers. Joan doesn't socialize with her neighbours, but this seemed like an important invitation and she wants to show support for the Neighbourhood Watch the Olivers are setting up. The break-ins have created a silent, unnamed force that will continue to bind these people together, though they don't really like each other much. They've not had dinner together before, these neighbours, not in this configuration.

Otto and Jerry are golf buddies. Debbie had been in the same book club as Grete, Otto's first wife, for fifteen years. Debbie invites Shelley and Otto to dinner once or twice a month, though she doesn't golf and she doesn't care for Shelley, either. 'The things you do for your husband!' thinks Debbie each time, usually finishing at least one gin and tonic before the Sommerfelds arrive.

After Steve explains that the Sommerfelds are fine, it's just that J. is visiting, that's all, Debbie turns to Joan, standing beside her, and says, "Shelley left her husband for Otto, you know. She was a maid at a hotel he ran." The topic of Otto and Shelley's romance is not new, but it has been a while since Debbie has had a new audience.

Joan hates gossipy women. "Well, do you blame her? I'm sure she wasn't working for fun."

Easy for her to talk, thinks Debbie; Joan doesn't have to spend time with people she doesn't like. Larry is the most antisocial person Debbie has ever met. And Joan does whatever pleases Joan, everyone knows that.

"You do know that Shelley left her two children to be with Otto, don't you? The youngest was only eight years old. Eight!"

"Debbie," Joan says, "how was that trip you and Jerry did in the spring—it was Italy, I heard, wasn't it?"

Steve watches the two women from across the room. Steve's always thought his friend Jerry's wife was like an animal you could as easily lead to the slaughterhouse as to water. He admires Joan's handling of her, though he's not surprised by it. Joan is what he would call a "very capable" woman. He's heard she can hold her own, drinking with anyone, male or female, and that impresses him.

Debbie sips from her glass of Chablis and grimaces. Steve told her, when he poured it, that the wine was produced by the newest vineyard in town, the one owned by an ex-NHL hockey player, in which Steve invested.

"Oh, my," she says to Joan, "Steve shouldn't be serving this stuff to company! Come, Joan, while I exchange this for a good old gin and tonic." The women wander toward the

sideboard, where Steve can hear them. He listens to Debbie talk about the Tuscan vineyards, the fresh pasta, and the handsome tour guides.

Joan stands a foot taller than Debbie and is very slim for her age. Good legs, from what he can see of them; he likes a strong calf, the hollow between the soleus *and* fibularis brevis *clearly differentiated. Steve raises his eyes to look at Joan's profile, her cheekbone similarly carved out, and is reminded of someone. Who does she look like? Where have I seen her before? She is so familiar, standing there, her elbow bent, a drink in one hand, the other lightly touching Debbie's back. Classy.*

"Jerry," Steve says later, his hand on the other's forearm, "whatever you do tonight, Jerry—Jerry, are you listening? Jerry, please, I ask just one thing: do not tell us about you and the Exxon settlement!" Steve laughs, looking around the room to see who is listening. Deal?"

"Don't pay any attention to him." Janet pats Jerry's other arm. "You can talk about anything you like in this house. But first do me a favour and call Otto, would you Jerry? Find out why they are so late." Jerry isn't sure what to say to that, but then Steve takes over, says he was joking about Exxon, and pulls him away from Janet.

Once the group is seated at the set table, Janet brings out a platter of chicken and a bowl of green beans. (The baked potatoes are still in the oven, wrapped in foil, where they will become hard and blackened.)

"Folks," Steve says abruptly, "I want to tell you about David Richardson." The guests are puzzled but no one wants to admit not knowing David Richardson. "My buddy Dave, he went to the Big Apple a couple of months ago. But he never came home."

"Ouch," says Jerry, quietly; he's heard this one before. Joan is next to Jerry and watches him reach for his wine glass. Turning to her, he says, *"This is gonna be a long night!"*

The men are obviously friends, thinks Joan, but she isn't sure why. She suspects Jerry is nouveau riche. *She's right. Jerry grew up in northern Saskatchewan and put himself through university one summer job at a time, until he won a scholarship that kept him going through a PhD in economics. If Jerry hadn't made several million consulting in the oil industry, he'd never have met Steve, the son of a Toronto surgeon who went from a private boys' school straight into pre-med.*

"Dave was.... He was a great guy." Steve hoists his glass in the air, but before he can think of a toast, Janet touches her husband's hand.

"Dave was Steve's best friend in medical school," she says gently.

"We shared a cadaver in anatomy!" Steve slams a fist on the table. "You can't get much closer than that!"

"We never saw them much," Janet says, "but still, it's a shock. He passed away at a jazz club. The nightmare his wife went through, getting his body—"

"His wife? What about Dave?" Steve was not usually argumentative, especially with Janet, no matter how much he drank. "Talk about a nightmare! Collapsing face first on the table, in front of strangers... with a saxophone blowing in your ear."

Janet changes the subject. "Dessert, anyone?"

"Umm, perhaps we could eat this lovely meal you've prepared for us first, Janet?" Debbie pours a glass of table wine for herself and tops up Jerry's. "This is a better vintage, Steve, than the Chablis you poured earlier."

The dishes are passed around, plates are filled with chicken and beans and salad. Steve quiets down, until Janet carries in a tray from the kitchen holding eight small plates, each with an individual puff pastry topped with whipping cream.

"What are you doing?" he yells.

Janet freezes, looks at the dessert.

Debbie intervenes. "Those look delicious, my dear! Just put that tray down on the buffet, Janet, till we're ready for them."

Joan looks at Debbie in profile—nose slightly upturned, no neck or chin definition to speak of—and thinks, Miss Piggy, that's who she reminds me of.

It's the end of the evening, and Debbie and Jerry Oliver are saying goodbye to Janet at the front door with Joan not far behind. Steve is suddenly beside her. He closes his fingers around her left wrist. He leans toward her right ear. "Tell me, Mrs. Palmer, haven't we met somewhere before?"

After dinner, Shelley pulls out family photo albums.

"Are there any pictures of your relatives in Germany, Pop?" J. asks, laughing as he looks at me.

"Show Sam the Kitchener pictures, Shelley," Otto says. Then he turns to me and starts talking.

"We did our time, Grete and me, running the upholstery business while the kids grew up. But—" he taps his index finger against his temple "—you're always better off if you can buy real estate. I invested as soon as I could. Farmland, apples and peaches. I hired managers to run them, and *they* found the workers. Not like now, with the government setting up programs to bring guys here from the third world. We had men from around *here* who wanted to work, and we treated them fine. For years, they were like family, those guys.

"Then I got lucky—apples and peaches were out, grapes were in. Everyone wanted the orchards cut down. But the grapes around here, remember Baby Duck? Those grapes were good for nothing but gut rot. I couldn't believe what they paid for the land. These new guys, I thought they were crazy, but they smartened up, they got the Europeans to educate them."

"And now they're such big shots," Shelley says, "they pretend they're living in Tuscany. And they sell most of their wine to China! The Chinese will be buying out the owners soon."

I glance at J., who mouths, "Again with the Chinese?" Trying not to laugh, I turn back to the album on Shelley's lap.

"We have lots and lots of pictures from Kitchener," says Shelley.

"Yah, lots of us moved here after the war," Otto says. "For a new start. Me and Grete had to work as farm hands for some German Canadians first. The Schenklers. I went from being a landowner to a farm labourer! We had to stay to repay the Mennonites for bringing us over. We were lucky to find a sponsor, we had no money, nothing. I worked hard to get us out of that situation, believe you me. It took a year for me to repay the price of our tickets, $548."

"You flew?"

"*Nein*, we came on a Canadian Pacific freighter called the 'Beaver Brae'—that's a name I'll never forget. It took corn and fruit to Europe, and they put in bunk beds down below to bring us emigrants back on the return trip. Eleven days, it took, to get to Quebec City. And then to Kitchener. Well, we survived.…

"But poor Grete, she was a city girl, you know[11]—

---

11 Grete wasn't in the family apartment in Berlin to witness Russian soldiers raping her mother on the kitchen table. She'd been sent to stay with well-off relatives in Dusseldorf while her mother waited for her father to come home from wherever he'd disappeared to, on business. They'd learn later that he had shipped himself out of the country by hiding in a coffin. He didn't come back for them.

she wasn't cut out for our new life, living in a wooden shack with no plumbing or electricity. Just two-by-fours and cedar posts, and a Franklin stove for our kitchen and heat. The bathroom was an outhouse, just a bench with a pail underneath it. One day the farmer told her to get rid of a crow hanging around the chickens, but she didn't know what to do, so I herded all the chickens into the coop. Then I took a leg from the chicken Grete made for lunch—which I hated to do, believe me—and I rubbed rat poison under the skin. 'When the crow eats this,' I told her, 'it dies. Then you put a pail over him, and I'll do the burying later, when I get back.' So she watched out the window, and when the crow finally ate enough and dropped to the ground, she went out and put the pail over it, like I told her." Otto laughs a little bit. "But then I'm out with the farmer, getting animal feed, and we're late coming back, so Grete decided she would bury the thing herself. When she lifted up the bucket—" Otto is now laughing so hard that he has to stop to catch his breath "—when she took it up, the crow flew straight up in the air! She dropped the pail, and she started screaming bloody murder!" Otto coughs up some sputum and takes a tissue from his pocket to spit into. "When I got home, I saw a dented bucket and a pile of vomit next to the chicken bone!"

It seems Shelley has heard the story many times before. Just before Otto's laughter triggers a coughing fit, she gets up and stands behind him, leans him forward, and slaps his back until it stops.

"Not many laughs in those days, though. I thought I'd be a treated like a fellow German by Schenkler, but we were more like slaves, Grete and me. The families that sponsored us came here in the 1800s, so they were *Canadians*, not

Germans anymore, you see."

"Like *my* people," Shelley says.

"There are a lot of Germans around Upton, too," J. says, looking at his grandfather. "You ever notice that wherever there are Germans, there aren't many Jews?"

But Otto doesn't hear him, or pretends he hasn't heard.

"Ach, you have no idea what it was like to be looked down on. We lived in a twenty-four-square-foot shack across the dirt road from the farm. Me, Grete, and we already had little Johnny then. A shack on a farm, with a pail under a bench for a bathroom! But what choice did I have?"

"Do you have any pictures from that time?"

Otto looks at J. as if he were an idiot. "Pictures? You think we had time to take pictures? Let alone money for film? Ach! You young people, you know nothing."

"The war made it hard for German families in Canada. My grandfather, he changed our family name from Schmidt to Smith, because of the prejudice," says Shelley.

"That was after the *First* World War, he did that." Otto doesn't pretend patience with his wife, but she seems oblivious.

"Oh, right. Anyway, my uncle was old enough for National Registration in the Second, and he died fighting the Germans. So, no one could say our family approved of what Hitler did!"

"My friends, Grete's and mine," Otto says, "the Schwartzwalds, Dieter and Hannah. They changed their name too, to Blackwood, when they came over. They were on our ship. You say 'Blackwood,' now," Otto keeps on, looking at me, "and no one thinks about where the word comes from. Their kids grew up and married and changed their name, anyway. Janie is Janie Harrison—there's no German in that, at all—but better than their

Mary. She married a guy named Chen! Dieter wasn't happy, but Hannah said, 'look at it this way, at least he's not Jewish!'"

J. stands up, looks at me as if to say, "let's scram," and says good night over his shoulder.

Shelley gets to her feet. "Let me put fresh sheets on that bed, J.," she says, following him. "No arguing. It's no problem, it's what I do."

Otto is quiet until he shifts in his chair. "Oh, that hurts!"

"Can I get you something?" I ask, standing up. "I have Tylenol in my purse."

"No, I'm fine. Thank you anyways... Sam. Short for Samara? Such an unusual name."

"Shelley told you about my grandmother's friend, I take it?"

"I heard the story yes. And your grandmother—"

I don't know why, but I start to tell Otto the whole story. It feels almost like a competition between us, the laying out of family hardships. "My grandmother had my mother when she was eighteen. Her parents sent them to Canada after the war, because it was difficult for the family in Norway then, economically. It wasn't easy here either, but Besta—that's short for *bestemor*, or grandmother, in Norwegian—she was lucky, because she found room and board and a babysitter in one go, when she got to Sudbury. The landlady was Finnish. She practically raised my mother."

Otto nods, looks down. I watch him think and guess that he must be remembering the war, or his childhood.

"How old were you when the war started, Otto?"

"I was eighteen, barely a man, but I was so happy when war came.[12] Not because I wanted to fight, only to get out of the

---

12   Otto likes to think about how good it felt to be young. He decides to talk to this Sam woman. Why not? It was decades ago, all that happened.

stink-stye of our farm. We had too much livestock," he said, "too much to manage. We were just simple farm people. I was the oldest, so I was expected to keep it going after the war."

Otto tells me the fathers and sons in his family did not get along. It was spite, he says, not pride, that made his grandfather hold onto his son's inheritance for so long. "By the time Father took it over, in the mid-thirties, he was fifty years old. The arthritis was too bad for my grandfather to keep working, that's the only reason he gave it up. He had no choice."

"There were generations of farmers, then, in your family."

"Our land was all we had. And Father wanted to give it to me. But guess what? I hated farming!" We both laugh. "I had been to Berlin," he says. "I was smitten with the city, and Grete....

"I remember putting on my uniform for the first time. I had so many photographs taken—as if I'd won an award or a scholarship, maybe. I looked good! A crisp cut for my hair, a part down the middle like a knife put it there. That smile on my face. And why not? City and country boys together, it didn't matter. We were all the same. Such camaraderie. And respect. Discipline, but respect too. The uniform made us proud of ourselves."

Otto is quiet for a few minutes, and I let him think about what he'd just said.

"And the farm? What happened to your farm?"

"My brother, he would have run it, but—well, there was no farm to run anyway. It got burned down by the Russians, like everything else."

"Ah, but when you bought your farms in Ontario, you just had to wait until the right time, when they were worth selling."

Otto seems agitated by my comment. For a moment, he looks at me sceptically, as if he is trying to figure out whether I am praising his acuity or criticizing his greed.

"Well, I didn't do too badly," he says, waving his hands around the room. "Especially from where I started. But look at me now. Ankles so swollen I can hardly walk. And when I do, ach—the wheezing starts up. The wheezing! Like I've been shot in the lungs. Fighting for my life, that's how it feels. You can hear it, *nein*?"

I nod. In the quietness of late evening, I can hear the effort his body is making to breathe, just to breathe. Excess saliva is oozing from the corners of his mouth and bubbling when he exhales, making him look, I think, like a fish—like an old, wrinkled, smelly fish.

"I don't push myself these days. Not much. Not much pushing anymore." Otto looks at his lap, his large hands resting on his thighs. "This is what I hate about getting old," he says. "The weakness. The shame."

J. is standing in the hallway now, I see, his hands closed in a cup shape in front of his chest. "Sam, would you open the front door for me? I have to put this spider out."

I follow J. and stand behind him as he releases the daddy long-legs into the garden next to the porch. "Saving spiders? You're not going all Zen on me, are you?"

"Ha ha. It's just when you spend as much time as I do, being still, not to mention sober, you start noticing things. This guy was in the bathroom."

"Maybe it's a female, and you've just separated her from her offspring. They are all going to die now, thanks to you."

"Nice. Thanks for that, Sam."

"You're letting more bugs in, you know. They're attracted to the light."

J. closes the door and puts his arm around my waist for balance.

"I dreamed last night that we had a dog named Alfred,"

J. says as we make the slow walk to his room at the end of the hall. "He was huge. And he could talk!" When we reach the living room, we see that Otto is asleep.

Quietly, J. tells me that in his dream, I was driving the car and he was beside me, as usual, while Alfred was sitting in the back seat, telling us he was angry we didn't have any children for him to play with.

"That's weird. I mean, we don't even have our own cat. Maybe you're projecting Otto's personality onto Alfred," I say. "He's pretty traditional. And critical."

"That's an understatement. But I know he wouldn't push me to have kids when I don't even have what he calls a real job."

"Hey!" Otto calls out to them. "Are you talking about me?"

"Not really, Pop, don't worry. Go back to sleep," J. says.

TUESDAY

This morning, I'm off on a winery tour, one of the most popular activities people come here for. The town's promotional site makes the area sound like Tuscany instead of an agricultural zone in transition:

> Beyond the town, the pristine countryside spreads out, dotted with vineyards—their sun-drenched rows of grapes serving as enticing invitations to some of our region's best wineries.

It takes me several minutes to inch my VW along the clogged main street to reach the road out of town, the same road I took in on Sunday. As I sit in the left-turn lane waiting for a break in oncoming traffic, I look at the United Church on the corner. From my research, I know it is the largest of the three that served the farming population in the township; on the drive to Upton, I'd noticed its portable marquee sign, perched on an angle so it faces incoming traffic, at the edge of its cemetery. That day, it said, "WELCOME BACK, ANN JOHNSTON!" which I read as an announcement that Ms. Johnston had returned to the fold.[13] Yesterday the sign said, "Location Location Location!"—huh?—and today, "God Don't Call the Acquainted."

My mother Gudrun grew up having never read the bible, and I was raised without any belief in the existence of a bearded white man in the sky. Sigrid, my grandmother, had been a Lutheran in Norway, but as a single young mother with a funny accent in Sudbury, she wasn't accepted by the church crowd. (She wore a gold band to make it seem as if she'd been widowed, but she didn't know the custom in Canada was to wear wedding rings on the left hand instead of the right, as in Norway, so the trick did her no good.) On Sundays my mother took me to the library at the university, where she was a secretary, to load up on books for the week. "You have to study to win scholarships, Sam, so you can leave this place," she told me from a young age, so young that she upset me with her talk of us separating. I remember saying I would never want to leave her. "You'll see when you're older," she said. "You'll want to meet new people. And make good friends." As I got older, I wondered if she was waiting for me to leave home so she could start her own life, whatever that might look like. But she never complained about not having privacy in our apartment, about not having a social life. When we fought about mine, in my teens, she was, I thought, alarmingly satisfied with the small, tight world she'd created for us.

She was supportive when I decided to end things with my university boyfriend, Brad. How easy it had been between us while we were both studying Arts and Humanities, when our worries were almost entirely about grades and what courses to take the next semester. And how hard Brad

---

13   In fact, Ann is a staff member who had just returned from maternity leave.

had taken my insistence on our living apart. He'd wanted to move in to protect me, he said, from the bitch next door who played her guitar and sang, badly, all day. ("I'm a serenader!" she'd screamed when I complained that I was trying to study, and she let her toy poodle shit in the hallway in the winter.) Brad wanted to keep me safe from the drug dealer down the hall, too, whose clients would come and go in the middle of the night.

But my place was too small for two, I insisted, and neither of us could afford anywhere larger even if we pooled our money. He gave up his shared apartment after graduation and moved to his parents' basement in Markham. I kept my studio apartment on Dundas West for a while and took on extra shifts bartending to supplement my café earnings. He'd call once in a while and ask me to remind him what it was like to be a surface dweller. When I phoned him that fall (against Fern's advice) and said I missed him, that I'd changed my mind, he said no. "I have a policy," he said: "Once a breakup, never a makeup. You can't unsay what you said to me, Sam. I'd never be able to trust you again." I knew that he was right. And so was Fern; I'd just been lonely, and it had been selfish of me, reaching out to him that way.

I heard recently, through mutual acquaintances, that Brad had met a nice girl and married, and that they have two young children and a house near his parents. I thought how odd it was that information like that filters down from the web of people you've once been connected to, and how the news can land on you like a lead balloon, the impact sending reverberations through the air and into your cells, your bones.

At the winery, in the retail outlet, I announce that I am here for a private tour, but the woman tapping on her keyboard, who wears her dark hair pulled back into a tight ponytail and her eyeliner as dark as her black nail polish, only lifts her left hand to silence me until she is ready.

I shut my eyes for three or four seconds to calm myself, while the clerk continues typing. When she swings around to face me, she has a broad smile full of perfect, white teeth.

"Yes. And you are?"

"Samara Johansen."

"One moment please."

While the guide is being sought, I pick up a brochure:

> "Quality grapes flourish around Upton Bay because of the lake effect, which imparts a graduated warming and cooling effect on the environment. Our Estate produces wines that you would mistake for those of a Burgundy appellation—our vinifera rootstocks are custom-grafted in France, though the local terroir inflects our varietals with unique nose and finish that is purely ours.
>
> Tastings of all our major wines, from Pinot Noir to Cabernet Sauvignon, are always available. Join one of our multiple daily tours of the award-winning demonstration vineyard, to learn about our practice of viticulture. Or visit our patio seasonally for ideal food samplings that go well with our exceptional wines. We are the area's top destination winery for a reason!"

"Sam, I'm Jake. Let's go to the sample site, shall we?"

The forty-something-year-old man who greets me is friendly until I ask about seeing the actual vineyard. "Sorry, off limits. We don't allow visitors. It's a tough job out there, and it would be distracting and dangerous for the workers to have us walk through."

I'm disappointed but remind myself that I am reporting on tourist activities, and—if this is all the tourists get—well, fine. Jake chats at me, repeats the brochure content almost word for word as we look at the three planted rows in the demo yard. "Our stock is verified by certified ampelographers," Jake boasts, and I nod even though I've never heard the word before. "And it's meticulously tended," Jake says.

"By whom?"

"By the staff on our team, of course."

"And your migrant workers, are they part of this team?"

Jake doesn't miss a beat. "Absolutely, of course! Everyone at the Estate is part of the family. We treat our workers very well indeed. If we didn't, they wouldn't want to come back, would they? And our workers return year after year. You'll find, if you check your facts, that we have one of the highest retention rates in the industry."

"I'm not here to investigate your policies," I told him. "I'm writing an article to promote the area for tourists."

"Great! Well, then, is there anything else I can share with you about our winery?"

"I'd like to see the patio and perhaps taste one of your offerings with a cheese pairing, if that's okay. For the article."

As Jake seats me in the tented dining area outside, someone, a male voice, screams in the far field. I put on my driving glasses but can't detect any movement back there other than the white flags waving in the breeze.

"Sounds like someone is in agony," I say, but Jake is already walking away and through the doors back into the building, cell phone to his ear. The bus-tour guests seated at the crowded tables—who had momentarily fallen silent, at the cry—return to their conversation.

It's stop-and-go all the way from Evil Maple back to Upton Bay. I hadn't expected traffic to be that bad, not on a weekday. The humidity is climbing, and I'm very thirsty after sampling melted asiago on sourdough crackers with a Reisling.

I keep thinking about the screech I heard on the patio of the winery, and I realize I'd never heard a man scream before. In movies, maybe, but not in real life. Not even in Toronto.

When I finally reach Main Street back in town, I see two fire trucks and an ambulance with their lights flashing up ahead in the town square. To avoid them, I wend my way to Otto and Shelley's through streets I've not been on before. I turn left and immediately regret it: a cement truck in front of a large home is blocking most of the road, pouring a driveway.

In the massive side yard of the house, I notice a white, windowed shed the size of the camps my friends' parents had on Ramsey Lake, when I was growing up, and a rectangular swimming pool. How great that would feel right now, I think, diving into clear, cool, blue water! I can almost smell the chlorine. I remember inhaling the scent at the community-centre pool in Sudbury and associating it with freedom, with the lightness that a young teenager feels once summer starts.

Four labourers, shovels in hand, are ready to distribute the heavy concrete as it slopped from the spout and hit the ground. The men—Mexicans, I think—wear dark work pants but are shirtless in the heat, their pitch-black, sweaty hair swept back off their faces. The temperature is at least one hundred degrees out and they are being splattered with corrosive cement, but they're laughing together. The truck starts to pull out, barely missing one of the thick stone posts of the gate marking either side of the driveway, and I drive past the place.

J. is on the front porch when I reach Otto's house. A Mercedes is parked behind Otto's BMW, and I can barely fit my car.

I reach into the passenger seat for my tote and slam the door, but it bounces open again. "Damn this door! It gets like this in the summer. As if the metal latch is swollen, or something."

"So much for German engineering," says J. "Personally, I'm against anything Volkswagen, on principle."

"I haven't heard you protesting when I'm driving you around, J."

"I guess you didn't have a good day?"

I sit down in the chair next to J.

"The winery tour was kind of depressing. I can't explain it, but the way people go wild for boutique wine—boutique anything. The overindulging, you know?"

"The entitlement."

"Exactly. Without a thought to how anything gets made. By people who are taken advantage of, usually." I look at J. "What? That's a smug look you're giving me."

J. shrugs. "It's good to be able to talk to you about this place. You didn't want to hear about it before, when I tried to explain how I felt about coming back here."

"You just went on and on and on, J. Admit it. Anyway. It was a bad day, I guess. I heard this man screaming, in the field behind the winery's retail centre. It was upsetting."

"They took you into the field, on the tour?"

"No. I asked, but they wouldn't let me in—no one goes

into the *real* vineyard, apparently. They just get a talk in front of a miniature set-up they call a 'Sample Site.'"

"I'm not surprised. They don't want you to see the horrible working conditions. Bad for business."

"Let's go inside—I've been in the sun all day."

"Okay, but I have to warn you, friends of Otto's are here. Janet and Steve. They're gossiping in the kitchen about the fire in my father's restaurant."

"Oh no! That explains the trucks and the ambulance I saw on my way back. Is it serious?"

"No," says J. "Not as bad as the last one. He's off the hook, good old Dad."

I give J. my right hand, and we grip thumbs so that J. can pull himself up. I open the door for J. and follow him in.

Otto is telling his audience that he thought he'd smelled something burning before he heard sirens.

"Shelley told me I was just being critical of her cooking, as usual! She had a strudel in the oven. But when we went to the front porch, we saw black smoke floating above the stores on the far side of Main. I never thought it would be John's place, though."

"I called him right away, of course," Shelley says. "The place is still standing. It was only a kitchen fire and the chef put it out very quickly. Good thing, too, because John said it took those trucks ages to get there! Imagine, all the taxes we pay, and still we have to wait for firemen to get here all the way from the city. Through all this traffic!"

The woman, Janet, turns toward J. and me as we stand listening in the doorway.

"J.! I haven't seen you since you were about five years old!"

Her husband reaches out to shake J.'s right hand, tapping his shoulder with the left, and whispers, "Never mind, just ignore her."[14] Then he turns to me.

"Steve Desmond, nice to meet you. This is my wife, Janet. We're old friends of Otto's."

Janet clasps my hand and covers it with her left, and I see a hole on the arm of Janet's cardigan that has been repaired, it seems, with glue.

Steve, who is clearly drunk, reminds me of J. when he used to drink into the night. You can get away with that less and less as you age, I think.

"You missed all the excitement," J. says to me. "I did too. I slept through the whole thing!"

"If only I could have!" says Steve. "I was having a nap, and I was confused and tried to pull the cord to the alarm clock out of the wall."

"Using a pair of old forceps," Janet adds. "Really, he keeps them on the nightstand, so he can reach the things he knocks off the table."

"Listen, how is Brian doing?" J. asks the Desmonds, but Janet looks confused. She seems to be trying to remember who J. is talking about.

"Not so good," Steve says. "We've not told many people, but Brian has had a brain tumour for some time. Inoperable."

"How could you not tell us that?" Shelley's voice rises, and she starts to tear up.

"Shell, it's benign," he explains. "But the pressure on his nerves causes seizures and makes him erratic and moody. We pay his rent and send him money, of course. I don't know how our kids turned out the way they did, with parents like us."

---

14   Janet had seen J. every summer until five years ago, when he stopped visiting Otto and Shelley regularly.

"Your daughter is successful!" Otto protests. "She's a lawyer, J., a lawyer in Toronto."

"Yes. Well, Linda has a wife named Orchid who is a landscaper in the summer and a bodybuilder in the winter."

"I had my appendix out on our honeymoon! Remember, Steve?"

Silence.

Otto asks Shelley to get Steve another beer, and J. asks me if I'd like some white wine. "Pop has only the best—Black Tower, good German wine."

I laugh and accept the bottle of beer Shelley offers me. "I hadn't seen a Löwenbräu in a long time, until you gave me one on Sunday. I used to bartend in university, and it was popular back then."

Otto shrugs and says, "It's still the best. The crap they make around here these days—with fruit in it, apricot, or raspberry—phttt! The guy I sold my land to makes pear-flavoured wine even. In my day, people wanted tradition. Eh, Steve? You know quality when you taste it. If these entrepreneurs with the micro this, and micro that—"

"It's all about giving people what they want, Pop. It's called progress."

"Excuse me, all, will you?" I say. "I need to take a shower, if that's okay."

"No permission needed, Samara, you know that." Shelley is so much friendlier to me, with other people around.

"Samara, what kind of a name is that?"

"Steve, don't be rude."

"How is being curious rude?"

"Never mind," Janet says. "It's J., right? Tell me, J., how are you related to Otto?"

"That's it," Steve says, taking Janet's wine glass. "You're cut off!" They all laugh.

"Samara is a Russian name," J. says, "but Sam is half Norwegian."

"Well, it's very pretty—Russian, Norwegian, or whatever," says Steve. "Listen, we should go. See you at the club tomorrow, Otto."[15]

"God willing, yes," Otto says.

"Pop, you're still wasting my inheritance on that club membership, huh?"

Janet smiles vacantly as she asks, "Are you and Shell coming to the Scottish Society on Friday night?"

"The Scottish Society?" J. says. "Pop, you can't pass yourself off as Scottish!"

"It should be called the *Scotch* Society," Steve says. "We do a lot of tasting and drinking single malts, and whoever guesses the correct label gets to take the bottle home."

As Otto walks Steve and Janet to the door, he tells them a Chinese couple knocked yesterday, asking if they could take their wedding pictures on the front porch.

"When I said no, they wanted to know why, so I told them, 'You can't afford the fee!' I was just joking, but they went away."

"Otto the diplomat," J. says.

"What, you want pictures of our house sent all over China?"

"They happened to be Japanese, Pop. I saw them."

"Whatever."

---

15 Otto meets Steve, Jerry, and Irv in the clubhouse after their game every Wednesday and Friday for lunch. He can't golf any longer—other players began complaining that he was so slow, he was holding everyone else up; but he stopped playing only when he soiled himself without noticing. Neither Steve nor Jerry said anything to him—a waitress made a joke about the wet spot in the restaurant, before opening a large serviette to cover his lap.

WEDNESDAY

A ringing phone wakes me up. My plan is to meet the publicity manager at the theatre after the matinee has started, so I let myself sleep in. For a moment I forget where I am, until the ornaments on the bookcase next to the window come into focus: two beer steins glazed in dark brown and cobalt blue; several carved wooden figurines, elderly rural folk grouped as if in conversation; a heavy ceramic vase, serving no purpose; three photographs of John and his sister when they were children, in tarnished silver filigree frames. The dark-blue curtains are not completely closed and there is a slender slit between them, so a sapphire-tinged dagger of light lies across the white bedspread, warming my feet.

Then I remember that yesterday, John's restaurant caught fire. Otto and Shelley don't seem to think it suspicious, but J. does.

After some coffee in the kitchen, we leave to have lunch at a bistro close enough to Otto's home that J. can make it on foot. We pass by a small cemetery with a historical plaque next to the sidewalk:

> The Negro Burial Ground was once the site of the town's Baptist Church formed in 1830. People from the congregation rest in the ground here.

"The government put the word 'negro' on its official plaque?" I ask.

"'Negro Burial Ground' is the historical name," J. says.

"I thought this area was part of the Underground Railway for slaves escaping from the States."

"It was. People here were liberal minded, for their day—"

"And that's the best they could do? Provide a small roadside cemetery? I only see three headstones."

"Maybe only three families could afford headstones. Or maybe only three stayed long enough to die here. There isn't a Black population here now, that's for sure. Not a single family."

"It's hard not to notice how white Upton Bay is."

"Last night Pop told me he sees at least one Black person on every news station he watches now, and he thinks he is being modern when he says how well-spoken they are."

"Man, he's unbelievable."

"My father told me once that when Pop went to Toronto on business, sometime in the sixties, I guess, and he stopped at an automat for a quick lunch—but when he saw a Black hand reach in to put a piece of pie into a slot, he lost his appetite and walked out without eating."

When we reach the bistro a young girl greets and leads us to a table, leaving menus for us to browse. The restaurant is crowded, and the ambient noise makes conversation difficult.

"Sam," says J., leaning forward, "I need to tell you something."

"You don't have your wallet with you, I know."

"I'm serious."

J. tells me that he suspects John of having started that fire yesterday, to collect insurance money. He says it wouldn't be the first time; when J. and his mom lived in town with John a few streets north of Main, their house burned down one night while they were visiting Otto and Grete. It was a century house, like most houses in "Olde Towne," but the wiring had been updated.

"The adjusters didn't find any signs of tampering, but Mom wasn't so sure. That's why we left." J. goes on to say that his mother couldn't stand to live with John after that. She couldn't keep any more secrets, she said, and she was worried about her and J.'s safety.

"Why? Did he take out life insurance policies on you both?"

"He took one out on my mother, I know that. He used to say she wouldn't live long, at the rate she was drinking, and he was right. He was the benefactor, even though they were divorced by then."

J. was in a college music program as a mature student in Ottawa when his mother died. He didn't go back home to attend to her funeral, something I have a hard time understanding. I imagine the regret that will land on him later will be much worse than the ambivalence he probably felt at the time.

"And there was something about Pop's finances before that. From what Mom told me, I think Dad ran a pyramid scheme or something and lost a lot of my grandparents' savings."

"If that's true, then your grandfather has done well since. He's hardly poor, is he?"

"Well, there was family money on my grandmother's side that my dad couldn't get at. That reminds me, I can't figure out what happened to my grandmother's painting, the one I mentioned before," J. says. "I was always told it was extremely valuable. It was by some artist from Vienna. You'd think Shelley would want to show it off—not that she's a connoisseur, or anything."

"If it came from Grete's family, Shelley might have taken it down. Maybe she feels second best, compared to your grandmother."

"Yeah, maybe. My grandmother was something else," J. says. "She was vain and didn't want anything to draw attention to her age. My cousins and I were forbidden to call her anything but 'G.M.' She said it was for Grand Mother, but we called her the General Manager behind her back. She was much tougher than Otto. Very German."

"Anyway, I wonder how Grete's family got the painting. Do you ever wonder?"

J. admits he hasn't thought about it. "Her family was from a higher class than Pop. He kind of worshipped her father, I think. His money, at least."

"Hmm. Do you know what Grete's last name was, before she married?"

"I think it was Lippert.[16] Why?"

"Because her brothers and male cousins would have been in the military like Otto. I've read a lot of articles lately about the third generation after the war finding out what

---

16 Grete's ancestors include Friedrich Lippert, 1780–1860, who served for a time as Burgermeister of a town (which no longer exists) named Singelbach in Hessen, once part of the Kingdom of Westphalia. Grete's relation to Julius Lippert—member of the Nazi Party from 1927, commander (then SA-Gruppenführer) of the SA–Gruppe Berlin-Brandenburg from January 1934, and Berlin's Oberbürgermeister and Stadtspräsident (City President) from 1937 to 1940—is not known.

their grandparents did and taking responsibility for their ancestors. With a little research, you could probably find out what roles Otto and your great-uncles played."

"So could you, about your own family." J. sounds defensive. "Norway wasn't perfect, you know. Germany didn't have a hard time taking over the country. The king and the government of Norway just took off, leaving the population to deal with the occupation on its own."

"J., they would have been executed otherwise. At least the Norwegians built a resistance. And I've told you about how my grandmother tried to save her friend from the Nazis. Your family, on the other hand, might have *been* Nazis."

"You don't know anything about your grandmother's past, you've told me that yourself. You're always talking about Norway as this place of great social justice, but that's only now, because of the oil. Wealth *allows* people to have empathy."

"Really, that's what you think? Then why are the rich people I've come across in this town so far not very nice to those who have less than they do?"

"Because basically, Sam, *everyone* is horrible. The winery guys, my dad, your grandparents and mine. Even the Mexican migrant guys probably look down on the Jamaican guys they work with in the fields. It's human nature. Everyone needs someone to hate."

"I don't."

"Yes, you do! You can't stand the rich!"

"That's different. I don't like their behaviour, the way they treat people who aren't in their so-called class."

"Are you talking about migrant workers? Because to be honest, I think they're lucky to get the jobs here. They can't make money back home like they do here. So, it's a win-win."

I close my eyes and shake my head. In the few days that J. and I have been in Upton Bay, I've noticed him shifting, slightly and bit by bit, away from his usual opinions.

"Let's not fight," J. says quietly, touching my hand. "I want this to be a happy occasion."

From his back pocket, J. pulls out a small, navy-blue box with a slim white ribbon, its ends spiralled, tied once around its middle. "It's our anniversary. Bet you didn't think I'd remember."

I blush, but not for the reason J. thinks. I am embarrassed because I hadn't paid attention to the date, and because it seems to mean a lot more to J. than I expected. The only times I have counted the weeks or months that I've been with J. have been when I've gotten tired of running loads of laundry to and from the local laundromat.

"You shouldn't have bought a gift, J." I hesitate, then slide the ribbon off the box and remove the lid. "Where did you get the money for this?"

"That's not a very nice way to say you like the bracelet."

"It is lovely." I put the silver bangle on my right hand. "But I still want to know how you managed this."

"I didn't go to the store. I know Max," J. says, "the jeweller in town. His son was a friend of mine when I lived here. I just called him and asked him for a suggestion. He delivered it while you were at the winery."

"On credit, then."

"You *know* I don't have an income at the moment."

J. must be feeling better, I think, since he is now so capable of irritation.

"Look on the inside of it."

I take it off again and see something written in tiny script, sized to fit the narrow width of the metal. I squint and make out my name and J.'s, with a date that must be the six-month mark that he wants to celebrate. And there's a number authenticating the material—925, for sterling silver—with the word TAXCO stamped next to it.

I start to thank J. but am interrupted by the entrance of two women who sit at the table behind us, speaking loudly.

"I'm so angry, Caroline! Now the entire *room* has to be repainted. And I cannot live with that kitchen as is, either—it's *so* outdated. But Fred says he won't pay for a full reno. He'll pay Sandy to resurface the cupboards, but that's it."

"Handy Sandy? Doesn't Fred know what he's like? He gossips all day and takes forever to do the simplest of chores! Mitch likes him for some reason too. But we pay Sandy more for *talking* than for working, I'll tell you that."

"What's Sandy short for, anyway?"

"I don't know. It's a girl's name."

"I'll never forget the morning he walked into the kitchen with his handwritten invoice. Hand printed, I should say, like a child's writing. I was about to have breakfast and all the cutlery was in the dishwasher, so I was using a steak knife to butter some toast, and he said it looked sharp—and then he launched into this story about his sister's birth! I was just about sick to my stomach!"

"I know, I know," Caroline says. "His dad was a butcher, his mother went into labour and the baby popped out, no time to get her to the hospital, so the man severed the umbilical cord with the knife he used to hack apart carcasses. He finds a way to insert that story into conversation with everyone he meets, as if it will make *him* seem—oh, I don't know—more manly or something."

The two women laugh loudly, slapping their hands on the table and leaning forward as for support, their mirth is so great.

We hurry through our lunch of cold corn chowder and a spinach side salad. Nothing could have been grown locally, I don't think, since all farmland for miles and miles has been converted for growing grapes. I jot down some notes about the food, for my article, on the back of the receipt.

Outside I take J.'s arm to support him until he finds his feet, and we soon pause in front of the window of the Bayside Gallery.

"That's Janet's work, I think," J. says.

"Really?" The signature in the bottom right corner indeed reads "J. Desmond," and it is dated 1998. The card says it is called "Peonies in a clear glass jar."

"A child could have done that," J. says. "Wait, no—my *unborn* child could have done that."

"J., stop," I say, but I am laughing. "It's actually quite good. I guess she was more cogent in 1998 than she is now."

"She was the director of another small gallery, once," J. says. "I used to have a sort of crush on Janet when I was a little kid. She was beautiful and calm, which my mother was not. Compared to my house, which was a pigsty, the Desmonds' was like another planet." Steve had the ego of a surgeon and slept with as many women as he could, J. continues, but their weekend home in Upton had a veneer J. found attractive. "One day I noticed that she never displayed her kids' schoolwork on the fridge. Brian said it was because it didn't go with the design and colour scheme she'd used in the kitchen. I think he found that hurtful."

"And now Brian has a brain tumour," I say, "and Janet seems to be losing her mind. So much for money buying happiness."

J. says he feels sorry for Steve.

"For Steve? What about Janet?"

"Of course I feel sorry for her. But she isn't exactly aware of what's going on, is she? I mean, a certain lack of awareness can be useful, that's all I'm saying."

I shake my head. We aren't seeing things the same way, but J. seems to be as oblivious to what is happening between us as Janet is to her own situation. I think about his perspective on our relationship, and my own—so different from his past girlfriends', all of whom, he's said, were looking for some form of permanence, which J. had never encouraged. I remember him telling me he thought I was like a guy, in that I was not possessive, and that excited him. Now he's working up to offering commitment to me, I think, feeling the bracelet dig into my flesh where J.'s weight is pressing against my forearm.

I remember how we used to be ravenous for each other, J. and I, before he got sick. Sex was probably what kept us together in the beginning. Now that our physical relationship has all but died, though, I know the end of our time together as a couple is in sight.

I meet Susan Brownridge, the publicity manager at Bayside Theatre, at our appointed time. She looks askance at my casual cotton dress, my open-toed, flat sandals, and the plain tote bag on my arm when she walks across the lobby toward me. She is brisk during the interview and keeps on script: "Our shows sell out within hours of being announced; bookings at hotels and B&Bs are now being made into the next year, all because of the unique entertainment the town offers; international reputation; exquisite surroundings for discriminating tastes," etc., etc. With a broad smile, she sidesteps my specific questions, like:

- Do play directors have the authority to update or modernize the classics that are performed year after year?

- Do you have plans to put on any socially engaged work? Or anything more contemporary, perhaps?
- What is the Bayside Theatre's policy on diversity?

by making references to the one actor in *Guys and Dolls* who has "that gorgeous complexion," which he owes to his Pakistani mother; to the company's "respect for the original words and intent" of the playwright; and to "the universality of great art."

With time to spare after the interview, I cross the street and find an empty research table in the historical courthouse, which has been operating as the town's library branch for several decades. I am grateful for the cool, damp air inside of the limestone building. Even my batik-dyed, spaghetti-strapped sun dress is not cool enough for this sticky weather.

I pull out my notebook, but I can't seem to focus well enough to write coherent sentences about the theatre scene, from any angle, because I am still bothered by my conversation with J. at lunch. I'm not sure which disturbs me most: J.'s callousness toward migrant workers; his lack of interest in both the source of that missing painting he so loves and the wartime story of his German grandparents and their families; or the gift he presented to me, which I'll end up paying for when the invoice eventually arrives in the mail, back in Toronto.

So I close my laptop screen and ask the carbuncular youth at the information desk where I might find books about viticulture. When he stares at me, I say, "The process of growing grapes for the purpose of making wine—you know?"

"Oh, *wine*." He types something into his computer (not viticulture, I am certain—I'd have had to give him the spelling for that to happen) and points to the second floor. "Anything we have will be upstairs," he says, then hands me a slip of paper with a Dewey decimal call number on it. "It's probably some dusty, ancient textbook. You should just Google it."

Irv, Steve, Jerry, and Otto meet for a game

The weather this morning is perfect for golf—no wind, just a slight, cooling breeze, and a cloudless cerulean sky. The friends are meeting at nine in the morning as usual for their Wednesday round. Despite his limp and his portable walker, Otto is there on the green. He decided not to wait for them in the clubhouse at lunch time, which he usually does; he felt like some fresh air, he says to his friends, and he has already arranged for a cart. The clubs for Irv, Jerry, and Steve have been brought up from storage by the assistant golf pro and loaded in the back. Jerry will drive the cart and Otto will sit beside him, while Irv and Steve walk on ahead to the first tee.

This summer, Jerry has developed the annoying habit of staring at the ball at his feet for longer and longer while the other three, and the pairs behind them, wait for him to take a swing. His gait has changed, too: he shuffles very slowly, shifting his weight from side to side. Irv suggests, as he and Steve walk, that maybe they should let Jerry go first to get it over with; but Steve prefers that the rest of them take their turns before they suffer the agony of Jerry's near-catatonic performance.

"Is it Parkinson's, do you think, Steve?"

Steve shrugs his shoulders in response and Irv wishes he hadn't mentioned it. He is usually careful around Steve, whose mannerisms can be borderline aggressive—though Irv tries not to be paranoid. He knows that Steve and Janet entertain a lot, but he and Rita are never invited to their dinners.

(From the early weeks of spring, Steve has known what drugs Jerry should be taking; but he hasn't said so to his friends, because to do so would be to intervene in another doctor's business—professional code, and all that. He only nods when Debbie takes him aside during dinners or drinks, to give him the latest report after Jerry sees his family physician, Dr. Reinhart. "Reinhart's a good man," Steve says, "a good man," which is all Debbie needs to hear.)

The two men walk on in silence for several steps. Eventually they talk about the theatre schedule, and which plays, if any, their wives say they should see this year. Then Irv begins a story about the Canadian actor he worked with when he was a program director at the CBC in the 1970s.[17] The broadcaster was doing a documentary on the man, who had come to headquarters for an interview drunk, arrogant, and vitriolic. "His fake English accent was the worst I'd heard in a while," Irv tells Steve. "Rita makes fun of mine sometimes because hers is cut-glass British, whereas mine was built on top of German from age seven or eight. But that guy's makes me cringe. I think he's done too much Shakespeare and it's gone to his head."

Steve starts to select clubs from his golf bag. Irv doesn't take Steve's lack of interest in him personally; Steve behaves much the same toward the others in the foursome. Otto does, too, as far as he can tell. Sometimes—he can't help himself—Irv pictures Otto in an army uniform and imagines him posting the "Kauf nicht bei Juden!" notices on the window of his father's watch business in Vienna.

But Irv doesn't like to dwell on history. He was born Irv

---

17   The actor, elderly himself now, is to appear in *The Tempest* in town this fall.

Rosenthal in Vienna in 1931. He legally changed his last name to Randall when he came of age in London, England, in 1952. To Irv, it is worse to bring up the past and find that people don't want to hear about it; that would be too, too painful, so he doesn't bother trying to interest them. Besides, he still feels, now and then, a subterranean, silent threat that he can't explain. Like the time a few years ago when he and Rita wanted a waiver for a building permit, to have a slightly larger than standard gazebo built in their back yard, and their neighbour wrote in protest to council, just to be difficult. And the way those people on council looked at Irv—nothing he could pin down in words or deeds, but there was something in their eyes that reminded him of the faces in the streets of Vienna, when he was a boy and his world was being dismantled, measure by measure.

The gazebo was turned down. No, better not let the past influence your outlook—that's been his way forward, his whole adult life.

Otto and Jerry arrive in the cart as Steve is practising his swing behind the tee. Irv looks over to the other pair. Otto disembarks, and Irv sees that the old guy has peed himself again.

I stop in the powder room when I get back to the house and splash some water on my face. I see that J. had used the washroom in the past hour or so, because he hasn't flushed the toilet—one of his worst habits, which he developed when he was living with his last girlfriend; he'd get home really late after a gig and didn't want to wake her up with the noise, he told me, when I first complained about it.

"You are consuming too much caffeine, J.," I say when I push his door open and sit in the chair beside his bed. "Your pee smells like coffee again."

I admit it, I have a bear nose. One night earlier this summer, when J. opened the front door of our house after going out with a friend and I came to the top of the stairs to greet him, I could smell the Scotch on his breath before he'd taken a step.

"Your nasal cavity is like a molecule scanner," he says to me now. "Do you know how strange that is?"

"Strange doesn't automatically mean bad. Maybe it's useful," I say. "An evolutionary skill."

"Depends on which way you look at it, I suppose."

The word *anamorphosis*[18] pops out from somewhere deep in my mind, where it has lodged since I took an undergraduate art-history course. I'll have to look it up later to remind myself of its meaning. I can't stand not knowing things.

"Do you ever feel like you need to know everything?" I ask J. "Like, where do chipmunks go in the winter; or how did anyone figure out how to make eyeglasses? Or bread. Who invented bread?"

"Honestly? No. But here's something I do know." J. rolls up a section of the newspaper and puts one end on my chest, the other against his ear. "What's this?"

"No idea."

"It's the first stethoscope. I saw a show on PBS once about early medical inventions. The guy who invented this noticed it amplified the sound of a heartbeat."

"I didn't know that."

"No one can know everything, Sam. Diversification—it's what led to civilization. It's what lets me be a musician, and scientists do what they do, and you—do what you do."

---

18   *anamorphosis*: noun: a distorted projection or drawing which appears normal when viewed from a particular point or with a suitable mirror or lens. [Oxford online dictionary at lexico.com/en/definition/anamorphosis]

"I just serve coffee, J."

"But you are becoming a writer. Anyway, it's just an example."

"I don't know if I agree with you, about me being a writer. Or about diversification. If everyone does just one activity for a living, and depends on other people doing millions of other activities, so the economic system can keep going—"

"Are you talking about migrants again?"

"—then it's like we live in a bubble, without recognizing all the people who labour on our behalf, just to keep *us* afloat in our bigger, better bubbles. So we can pretend we're self-sufficient."

"You think it'd be better if we grew our own food, chopped our own wood? You're sounding like a survivalist or something now, Sam. You're scaring me," J. says, though he is smiling.

There. That's a perfect example of what I've been sensing—that the town is having an osmotic impact on J., as if, back here where he was born and where his father and grandfather have stayed, his cells have shifted their magnetic orientation one by one, producing a brand-new J. Or maybe it's the old J., the real J.?

Suddenly I feel fury toward him, and the anger triggers a memory of being fifteen in Copper Cliff, arguing with my mother about a boy. My date, whose family was Italian and whose father worked in the mines, was going to take me to the slag pile, where I'd never been: the glowing-hot, red-orange waste heap outside the smelter, which slowly slid to a stop and softly lit up a parking area where couples made out in their parents' cars. My mother didn't know about the slag pile part of our date, but she suggested that I date a different boy, someone with a future outside of our small town, which

I interpreted as racist. "That's rich, coming from you—you're an immigrant!" I shouted at her. Shouting was one behaviour my mother would not allow in our home, so to avoid a slap I ran into the bathroom, filled the bathtub, dunked my head, and screamed bubbles of outrage into the water. To the closed door, my mother said that she wasn't discriminating against anyone, she just wanted better for me.

Now I think about what J. said earlier: *Everyone needs someone to hate.*

J. looks at my hand. "Hey, you're not wearing the bracelet."

I scratch at my wrist, where the bracelet used to be. I'm not used to wearing jewellery. It gets in the way, whether tangling at your neck or pinching your finger or bouncing against your wrist bone. "Silver gets hot in the sun, you know. It's too humid today to have metal stuck to my skin," I tell J.

He nods. "I learned a bit about metallurgy from a girlfriend who took it in college," he says, then starts in on one of his monologues. "All metals come from minerals that combine with specific elemental molecules, and once early humans discovered copper and gold and silver, they used them to make weapons for hunting. Then," he says, "once people were well fed, and safe, metal came to represent wealth and rich people started using it for jewellery."

I don't prolong the conversation, but I know that J.'s version of history isn't right; pure metals were too soft to use for weapons. I'd read an article a few years ago about an archer's grave that was found in England near Stonehenge; archeologists knew before carbon dating that he was from the early Bronze Age, not the Stone Age, because there were copper decorations and gold hair ornaments in his tomb—no weapons or tools, just jewellery. Bling came first.

Later, in my room, I swallow three ibuprofen tablets for the pounding behind my right eye and a Gravol for my upset stomach. Without air conditioning—Shelley turns it off at night, saying it bothers her asthma—the house is a headache incubator, and even my arms feel nauseated. I lie down to wait for the throbbing to subside. Please, please don't start vomiting, I beg my body. I see the silver bracelet on the nightstand next to the bed, where I left it after lunch.

I pick up the bangle and run my finger around the inner surface until I can feel the stamped mark that says TAXCO, and I think about David, whom I met after Brad refused to reunite with me.

David and I once rented an apartment for a month in San Miguel d'Allende, Mexico, so he could take a spring-session sculpture class at the *Bellas des Artes*. Accommodation was cheap there, up in the mountains, because it was four hours north of Mexico City by bus, and even farther from a beach. Our rental, a second-storey flat, was owned by an American watercolour artist who was away teaching in Europe somewhere; the duplex was on a street where storekeepers, tailors, mechanical repairmen, and coffin vendors lived. Drug dealers, too. On the jagged glass-edged roof of the one-storey house next door, for instance, two pit bulls paced and barked and shit and ate and urinated, all day and night. This was our dealing neighbour's low-tech security system for alerting them to prying eyes (though not likely those of the *policia*, who were regular customers).

I loved the cool San Miguel evenings, when the open, screenless windows rattled in their wrought-iron frames as the night winds blew. David and I would sit on our own rooftop terrace, drinking gin and lemonade and listening to the sounds of the place: the restaurants catering to American ex-pats by playing Frank Sinatra and Dean Martin on outdoor speakers, the laughter of teens on the church steps, kissing under the planned parenthood signs. We went to the cinema one night, just a screen set up in the courtyard of a bar, where a bowl of popcorn was served with every martini. It was showing a Johnny Depp film that night—*Ed Wood*? Yes, *Ed Wood*, which David and I both loved. After the show, we walked back to the apartment and David tried on one of my silk dresses from India, made from recycled saris, the only clothes I'd packed in my carry-on knapsack.

I remember how David then rubbed my lipstick on his own mouth and kissed my nipples pink, and how we made love into the morning, to the sounds of the roosters waking the neighbourhood and the ting of triangles announcing the arrival of the garbage trucks at 6:00 a.m., when everyone ran to the street with their thin plastic bags full of rotting melon rinds and mango peels, empty Coca-Cola cans and *cerveza* bottles, chicken bones and sausage fat.

For dinner that whole month we ate mostly rice and beans; lunch consisted of fruit from the street vendors, chunks of watermelon and honeydew for two or three pesos. In the evenings, on TV we sometimes watched *telenovelas* in Spanish, in which the all-white cast cried, episode after episode, in hospital rooms and colonial-style homes. One day we bused to Guanajuato, to go to the Mummy Museum, where the bodies belonging to families who couldn't make the ongoing payments for burial were dug up and brought to the tourist attraction; they were remarkably preserved and dignified, even those corpses that had their genitalia exposed to reveal pubic hair and testicles. Before David and I returned to

Mexico City for the flight home, we took another second-class bus to Queretaro, sitting among the Maya women carrying wicker cages with chickens in them. There we rented a high-ceilinged room in an old palace on the *zocalo,* once grand but worn and noisy at night with American pub music playing from loudspeakers for the tourists, and where tiny, crab-like insects circled the base of the faucet in the bathroom sink. That night, David gave me a TAXCO-stamped ring, a memento of the trip, a consolation prize, before we separated at the end of our adventure.

I wonder if the silver in the bracelet from J. is from Queretaro. I can't remember what happened to the ring David had given me. I know what happened to *him* and why he didn't come back to me, in Toronto: he went back to Ellen, the woman he'd been with before we met. He told me he was going to BC to find Ellen, who was once his *raison d'être,* and if things worked out, I wouldn't hear from him again. I told him I am a strong woman, a Viking woman, and that I would understand if things were to end between us; still, it took me many months to put David behind me. My friend Fern, trying to cheer me up in the aftermath, referred to Ellen as The Raisin, and the laughter helped a little.

A tingle is starting on my ankle: this is how the relief comes to me, as a migraine starts to wane: one small patch of skin sends a chill from foot to calf and along my leg, then moves to my torso and arms, signalling a turn. It's a feeling on the surface, like goose bumps when you are cold, except I'm not—I am still coated with a light sweat from the waves of nausea that rolled through me for half an hour or more, before this welcome shift. Then I'm both hot and cold at the same time, and it's divine. I pull a sheet over myself, then throw it off again when I realize the time.

"Get up, Sam," I say out loud. "You have a lot of work to do."

Thursday, tomorrow, is the day I plan to draft my article and select the sites for pictures to be taken. But before I can write a word about tourism in this town, I have to go back to Evil Maple to ask about the injured worker I heard crying out in pain.

THURSDAY

Again, noise wakes me up earlier than I'd planned. I look out the bedroom window and see an ambulance stop in front of the house across the street, lights whirling and siren wailing, knocking over the three orange cones set in place on the asphalt. A few minutes later, I see an elegant woman with long, thin, strawberry-brunette hair and very pale skin, dressed in a satin-finish leopard-print belted bathrobe, open the front door; two paramedics come out of the house wheeling a covered body on a gurney down the front sidewalk to their vehicle. The woman closes her door before they drive quietly away, no siren sounding, no lights flashing.

In the kitchen, I say good morning to Shelley, who jerks the glass of orange juice she was holding to her lips, spilling it on her nightgown.

"God, Samara, you scared me!"

"Sorry, didn't mean to."

"No, it's my fault. I didn't sleep well. Otto is getting up five times a night to pee. I'm going to insist on a catheter, that's it. I'm calling the clinic as soon as it opens to have a nurse to come here. He won't wear disposable underwear and he keeps having accidents. He leaves me no choice."

"Um, okay," I say.

Then Shelley tells me that their neighbour Larry died this morning. The news has spread up and down the street by phone already.

"I saw an ambulance leave the house across the street earlier. That must have been him?"

"Unless Joan had someone *else* in there last night! Which is possible. Joan's been known to push things in that marriage, you could say."

Really? Gossip, now? About a just-widowed eighty-five-year-old? Shelley can't help herself, I think.

I reach for a mug, pour a cup of coffee. After four full days in this house, I have begun to help myself to whatever I need; Shelley seems to have given up her habit of pretending to be the happy hostess.

"Isn't Joan the woman you told me about, who wears sunglasses to parties to hide bruises from her husband's attacks?"

"There are two sides to every story, you know."

"Oh, at least," I say. Since Shelley, like Otto, takes most of my questions as rebukes, I've learned to counter with agreement. I'm amazed at how well it works.

"Just watch," Shelley says to me, her new confidante. "I bet by this afternoon, there will be a For Sale sign out front. Joan will want to cash in and move somewhere, so she can find another man." I nod and sip, nod and sip, while Shelley talks about Joan Palmer, then run upstairs to get dressed for my outing.

It's a cloudy day, and for the first time this week I feel a slight breeze in the air. I arrive at the winery before 8:00 a.m. Buses of ticket holders for the tour/tasting/lunch-with-wine package will soon be arriving from Buffalo and Toronto, but for now the parking lot is empty—other than the vehicle I'm guessing belongs to the cashier in the storefront, which opens at 7:30 a.m. for anyone who needs a bottle or two to get them through the morning.

I take a small notepad and a pen from my tote. I don't want to make small talk with the nail-polished clerk while pretending to browse, which seems fine with her because she goes outside to smoke a cigarette. I take the opportunity to slip out the back door and into the fake vineyard, from which I then wend my way toward the rows of vines, passing what looks like an abandoned, ad-hoc trailer park on the way there.

The sun is strong already and the breeze has disappeared. I see several people working in each long row of vines, which begin a few hundred feet from the store and seem to run into the horizon. The dense plants are tied to stakes and are at shoulder height, though most workers are bent at the waist, some crouching with their knees bent in front of them.

I am wearing sunglasses, but I forgot to take one of Shelley's hats, and by the time I reach the workers, I'm sure my forehead is already turning red. The crew of about two dozen is made up mostly of men, though I see two short women at the near end of one row who seem to be having trouble reaching the top of the taller plants.

"Hello," I say quietly, to the air, and several men stop and turn their heads to look at me, unsure what to do. *Is this woman an owner? An owner's daughter? A messenger?* I imagine them thinking.

"*Hola,*" a man of about forty says, approaching me from a row to my right. I think he must be the foreman.

"No *Español,*" I say apologetically. "English?"

He gestures behind his back, waving to the others who are standing still and watching, as if to say, "Get back to work." He holds his hand out to me, when he is close enough, and I shake it.

"Alberto," he says. No smile.

"Sam. I'm a wri—"

No. My instinct tells me that the word "writer" could sound threatening.

"I mean, I was going by in my car and just wanted to stop and say hello to that man, the one with the bandage."

Alberto narrows his eyes and turns his head just a little, judging me.

"I'm sort of a friend," I say. "I met him at the Valu-Mart in town on Sunday."

How easily the lie came to me! Foolishly, I hadn't planned what I was going to do or say here this morning; I was running on instinct alone.

"No trouble," Alberto says, and I am not sure if he means "no one has any concerns" or that he wants me to leave; but then Alberto does smile, slightly.

"Matias," he calls over his shoulder. "A friend of yours is here to see you." Then, pointing his finger directly at me, he says, "Not long. One minute, okay? Or I have problem. We all do."

I look at Matias as he walks forward, while Alberto walks back to the vines. Each man stares at the other's face until they pass one another. Alberto is now out of hearing range.

Matias wipes his forehead with the back of his hand. He is blinking sweat out of his eyes, breathing through his mouth. His T-shirt is stuck to his chest. It is 8:15 in the morning.

"I'm Sam."

Matias nods, hands on hips. I feel awkward because my right hand is extended, and Matias is not about to shake. I am self-conscious about my clean, perfectly shaped fingernails, so I start to cross my arms until I remember that this posture tends to shut people down, rather than open up conversation. I hold my hands behind my back, instead.

"Alberto has given me just minute to talk to you. I told him I'm your friend. *Amiga.*" David's intense effort to learn and teach me Spanish has left me with a tiny, dormant vocabulary that I am happy to rediscover.

We are standing only two feet apart, to keep our conversation as private as possible. Alberto is glancing at us between shouts to other workers.

"I could hear someone suffering, someone in pain, when I was here on Tuesday afternoon," I say, "and I came back to see if everything is all right."

"*Sí,* Tuesday." Matias's arms now hang at his sides. It's the right hand that is hurt. "And is Thursday, when you come?"

Touché. He has no reason to trust me, and I have no idea what I am doing here, really. My gut tells me something is wrong, that's all.

I can smell something fetid coming from Matias's hand, an odour that reminds me of how my own skin had smelled when the cast on my broken leg was removed, six weeks after the bone was set: like a room closed off for too long; like a sweet rot, that smell.[19]

I point to Matias's wound. "You might need antibiotics for that."

Matias shakes his head. He says nothing for a few seconds, as if trying to figure out what and whom I might be.

---

19 Sam was nine, spending the summer with her grandmother Sigrid in French River where she cleaned at Lift-the-Latch Lodge. Sam told the doctors she'd fallen off a bike, that she felt her shin snap when her shoe got caught in the leather foot strap, and that her head hit a rock, knocking her out. This was true, though she did not tell them that she had been fleeing her grandmother, who was coming after her with a broom, ready to beat her for backtalking.

I let him think, nodding and smiling to make it seem to Alberto that we are speaking to each other in a friendly, casual way.

"We can meet at the peaches, down the road. About nine." Matias nods and turns around to face Alberto and walks towards him and the others. When he reaches his co-workers, they start laughing, joking with him.

"*De nada, de nada*," I hear Matias say, unsteady on his feet as their hands push against his shoulders. Then Alberto yells, "Enough!" and they fall silent, gathering their tools and water bottles, returning to their work.

Back at the house, I find Otto in his usual spot in the living room.

"Hi, Otto," I say. "You know everyone around here, right?"

Otto smiles, nods.

"I was out at Evil Maple Estates today. What can you tell me about the guy who owns it?"

"Well, his father used to have a peach orchard. Dead now, but his son—Phil, I think his name is —he ripped out the trees to plant vines. He's a good kid."

"Really?" I feel my emotions rising in my throat, warning me not to continue. And yet. "Do you think a good person would force an injured worker to carry on doing twelve-hour shifts without medical care?"

Otto turns from the television and looks straight at me. After a second or two, he launches into a speech that sounds exactly like J. at lunch yesterday.

"Those men he hires have a good deal. They make more money here than they'd make in a year back home, and they get free lodging while they work. When I came here as an immigrant, a refugee, practically, I had it *much* worse. The shed we lived in! In the winter!"

"Yes, you told me. But Otto, you can't compare—I mean, you had a guaranteed future here, you could build—"

"I had to break my back here. That's the truth. I didn't inherit anything, like Phil did. I got nothing for free."

"Otto, that's not my point. I'm just saying—"

"No, please! Say nothing more to me today. I'm tired. Leave me be."

As I stood up, I looked at the burgundy-coloured wall next to Otto's chair, where J. insists that his grandmother's mysterious painting used to hang. There are many marks where nails were hammered in and pulled out, from Shelley's decorating over the years—her attempt at the erasure of Grete. Like chickenpox scars, some of them, where the plaster has fragmented and crumbled away, leaving crevices behind; others are dry lumps with faint vein-like cracks running from the puncture point back to the wall. Shelley must have cataracts, I think, leaving the flaws exposed this way.[20]

Upstairs I turn on my laptop and get to work googling.

> What do migrant workers do in Ontario vineyards?

One of the search results is a job posting from last winter:

---

20 It's age, that's all, this loss of interest. For much of her marriage, Shelley had insisted on hiring professional painters every five years to repair walls and change the colours of the principal rooms in this house. It's been a decade since she collected paint chips from the hardware store, sticking them in picture frames and taping them to furniture, to gauge their hue, and half of another decade since she tried to cover worn edges and scratches with close-enough coloured acrylics she found at the Dollar Store. These defects and disfigurements disgust Elisabeth, Otto's daughter, who will think about their impact on resale, when she comes to visit shortly.

Are you energetic? Do you take pride in your work? Because we are looking for a fabulous person to join our team that cares for fifteen acres of grapes! We are looking for someone who enjoys working outside in all weather conditions contributing to every aspect of vineyard operations throughout the life cycle of the vine, from spring pruning to fall harvest. Position is seasonal, paid hourly. Experience, reliable transportation, and passion for quality viticultural practices mandatory. Routine activities under the supervision of the Manager include: Canopy Management, Erosion Control, Fertilizing, Cluster Thinning, Harvesting and/or Sorting of Wine Grape, Hoeing, Tractor and Special Machinery Operations (Cultivator, Pre-Pruning Cane Cutter, Wind Machines), Leaf Pulling, Perimeter Maintenance, Planting, Pruning, Hedging, Root Removal, Shoot Tipping, Staking, Suckering, Weeding, Tying Vines to Trellises, Application of Various Spray Mixtures, Grass Cutting, Greenhouse Tasks, and other Winery Property Tasks.

The language of the ad and the capitalized task list makes the position sound sophisticated. There is no indication that long days and physical hardship is the norm. And how would migrant workers afford, or even find, "reliable transportation"? Where would they live?

 I find a couple of pieces on national newspaper sites about the federal program that allows migrant agricultural workers to live in Canada for up to eight months per year. I learn that the migrants must pay into the national employment insurance program, despite making minimum wage and not being eligible to collect EI themselves. The owners of the farms and vineyards in these articles are pictured and profiled as local heroes, and I instinctively dislike them, their white tanned faces smiling at the camera for the papers' photographers. Then I read some technical articles about the processes that vineyard workers follow in the course of completing their work, and I look up the meaning of the words in postings about the wineries in the area. I became fascinated by the vocabulary used by those in the business of growing grapes:

> **Bleeding**: when sap runs from an open pruning wound in early spring; this is a sign of health of the vine.

Yet when workers bleed, I thought, *they are not treated, to maintain the health of the bottom line.*

> **Callus**: After a vine is pruned, a callus forms over the wound.

And over the employers' hearts.

> **The Crush**: what harvest time is called in North America: grapes are picked and collected, then broken by a press.

The workload for migrant team members is twelve hours per day, six or seven days per week, enough to break the best of people.

Free run: the juice that emerges when grapes are mechanically broken and allowed to ferment.

Must workers be crushed before being set free?

Secateurs: one-handed clippers for pruning.

That's a classy-sounding word for a basic tool of labour.

Terroir: the characteristic of the land/environment where vines grow.

And only one letter away from the feelings of workers who are powerless, taken advantage of by the owners, the partakers of wine, the citizens of this town, this country.

A dog somewhere close by is barking itself hoarse in the heat.

"He's been barking all day," Shelley says when I ask her who owns the dog next door.

"He shouldn't be left out in this heat."

"Where are you going?"

"To talk to your neighbour. I don't know how you can stand listening to that noise." Especially since you're not deaf like Otto, I think.

"Sam, please! We have to live here, not you. Don't make trouble for us."

"Don't worry, I won't."

Outside, I look in the laneway along the side of the house toward where the noise seems to be coming from. Through the hedge I see a black Labrador Retriever sitting on its haunches at the side door of the house behind Otto's, a rope around its neck, tongue hanging from the side of its mouth, panting between barks. A water bowl has been tipped over on its side, the liquid long evaporated. I squeeze through the greenery and when the dog sees me, he struggles to stand, making some effort to wag his tail. I am touched at this desire to greet me, despite his obvious distress. I pet his head, say, "I'll be right back," then walk to the front of the house. The dog starts barking again as soon as I am out of his sight.

I press the doorbell button over and over, but no one comes, so I start to bang my fist against the screen-door window. Beads of sweat are forming on my upper lip, my hairline, my neckline, and more are running down my back. An ancient-looking bald man finally opens the solid-wood inner door and looks at me through the glass. I smile.

When I realize that the man isn't going to open the screen-door, I tell him in a loud voice that it is too hot for the dog outside today, that there is a heat warning.

"He *asked* to be let out!" he yells, his eyes squinting as if he can't see me clearly.

"That may be," I say, "but you can't leave him outside for hours in this heat." The man scowls and slams the inner door shut. I begin to imagine the phone call I will need to make to the humane society, when I hear a shaky voice calling out at the back door. When I get there, I see the dog's tail disappear inside the house. I take a deep breath and leave.

Irv has a secret

Irv drives to the Valu-Mart to pick up milk and cat food on his way home after the golf game. Rita and Irv have five cats but no children, for which they are grateful every time they hear the stories friends tell them about their offspring: the lesbian, the brain tumour, the financial catastrophes! Rita says acting was enough drama, for her.[21]

Irv doesn't really like playing golf, but he remembered his father complaining that the International Golf-Club, where the other business owners in Vienna played, would not let Jews join or even play as a guest. So ever since Irv started earning enough to afford the fees, he's been a member of a golf club to honour his father more than to indulge himself in the sport: first he joined the Bayview Country Club in Toronto, and then he joined Upton Bay as soon as he and Rita moved here.

Irv believes you need to exercise your rights, or you could lose them. "It's like voting," he told Max, one of the few other Jewish people in Upton, when he asked the jeweller if he wanted to play a round. (Max figures it makes no difference—you can lose your rights regardless, if a population goes too far to the right, so why pay money and spend time with a bunch of guys who bore you to death? But Irv married a goy, so there you go.)

Irv had been wary of leaving Toronto and his Jewish circle, the writers and directors he'd worked with for decades, when Rita decided they should retire to Upton Bay. She was drawn to its theatre culture (if you call clichéd musicals theatre, Irv thought to himself). But he'd sacrificed more than that for her before. His older brother Harold,[22] the only family Irv had left,

---

21 Rita and Irv met in 1960 at a West End production of *The Caretaker*. Irv was covering the show for *The Guardian*, and Rita spent every pound she could spare on theatre tickets. She wanted to act. "That's Act with a capital A!" she told Irv, her pale cheeks blushing pink as the two of them chit-chatted during intermission. Rita knew someone working at a new theatre company in Toronto who would give her a chance, and soon Irv found himself leaving London and marrying Rita at Toronto City Hall.

22 Harold also survived the Holocaust when he, Irv and their parents fled Vienna for London, after *Kristallnacht*. Harold was interned with his father after war was declared, while Irv continued his high-school studies at Bunce Court.

refused to keep contact with Irv if he married Rita; this was after Irv introduced Rita to Harold, and she referred to his kipah as "that Jewish thing" on his head. ("So what if she doesn't know the name of it?" Irv argued, but Harold wouldn't listen.)

As soon as Irv steps inside the store a bird sweeps past his head, swoops down, and lands on the shelf above the broccoli. It immediately flies to a rafter, then back down to the shelf, but this time it hits the wall and sits stunned on a cabbage for a couple of seconds, before returning to the rafter. Over and over, the bird takes off and returns, ignoring the bags of birdseed that lie stacked on the floor by the automatic sliding entrance door. It's a small, greyish thing that Irv thinks must be a white-crowned sparrow, like the ones that come to the bird feeder outside their living room window. Entertainment for the indoor cats, Rita likes to say, though Irv thinks it's more like torment.

"You realize you have a bird trapped in here?" Irv says to a man unloading apples from a crate onto a display table.

"This is day three," the man says. "He was right there at the exit door last night before we locked up, but he's too stupid to fly out."

Three days? The bird is distressed and probably hungry, thinks Irv.

"Isn't there a Humane Society, somebody you can call?"

"They won't come for a bird," mumbles the man, whose name tag says Peter.

Irv can't believe the employees, let alone the hundreds of people who come through the store every day, haven't done anything about this creature. Has no one else complained? On behalf of the bird, he means, though the bird poop on the produce is hardly appealing.

He asks Peter if he can speak to the manager and is told she is on vacation. The assistant manager, then?

"You're looking at him." The two men stand there staring at each other. Peter is shorter than Irv, but his arms are crossed and he has thrust his head forward on his thick neck. Something about his eyes reminds Irv of the bully at Bunce Court School in Kent, where he lived during the war. He remembers taunts of "Where's your dad, Rosenthal? Oh right, he's an enemy of the state, isn't that it?"

When Irv gets home, he looks up a couple of animal-rescue options on his computer. He also looks up the phone number for Valu-Mart's regional head office, then decides to take the cordless handset outside to the back yard to make his calls, as his wife's sympathies begin and end with cats. Rita doesn't hear him lodging his complaint about Peter, offering to pay for the rescue, or giving his credit card number to WAR, the Wildlife Animal Removal Company, which promised to release the bird safely into the treed area beside the parking lot. When the statement comes, if Rita notices the charge, Irv plans to tell her that he donated to the War Amps after taking a call from a persistent fundraiser. He'll hunt through the junk drawer in the laundry room to find one of those keychain tags he'd gotten in the mail, if it comes to that.

J. is in his room listening to a Led Zeppelin CD on his portable player. He yanks the ear buds out when he sees me walk by.

"Hey!" he calls to me, but I keep going. "Sam?"

"What is it, J.? I have to get back to my writing. I can't visit with you all the time."

"Come on, Sam! It's just a little tourism article for your friend. Come here. I want to tell you something."

Instead, I go back down the hall and into the kitchen for a glass of fresh, cold water to take upstairs with me.

Shelley is looking out the window again when I walk in, fill a tumbler from the tap, and turn to leave again. But Shelley wants to talk.

"While you were gone, Sam, there was more activity across the street. I saw Steve Desmond park his car and walk to her side door."

"Offering his condolences?"

"Yeah, I guess so. She is too old for Steve, even if she is young-looking for her age, which she loves to brag about. Last summer I heard Joan talking to Rose on the driveway while she unloaded some groceries. 'I pulled over on the side of the road to buy a few cobs of corn, and the young man just *refused* to believe I'm a septuagenarian, when I told him!'"[23]

I smile and tell Shelley I have to get to work. Shelley waddles down the hall behind me.

"Otto? It's time for your pills," Shelley says at the living room door. But Otto isn't responding. "Are you asleep *again*?"

Otto's head is resting against his shoulder at an uncomfortable-looking angle. "I'm too young for this," mutters Shelley, pulling a Kleenex from the box on his side table. She wipes at the saliva drooling down the side of Otto's chin. "Maybe it would be best for everyone—" She stops herself from finishing the sentence and I hear her sniffling.

I go back towards the living room and lean against the doorframe.

"I didn't think about all this, when we got married," Shelley says when she sees me. "Or about the problems with the kids. All those money problems with John over the years, all those questions that never seemed to get answered,

---

23 He didn't know what the word meant; also, she was already eighty-six by then.

the fight with him about Grete's painting... yet Otto adores him! He always believes John's version of the story. And then there's his daughter..."

"J.'s Aunt Evelyn?"

"Elisabeth. Some daughter *she* is. Even when her father was so sick, five years ago, she didn't care. After Otto's quadruple bypass surgery, she visited him just once. Once! And stayed for ten minutes!"

"That's terrible." I rub Shelley's back a little.

"I called her a few weeks ago and told her about all the laundry I have to do for him, now that he is practically incontinent. Just so she'd know what was going on. Now, out of the blue, she calls this morning and says she is going to take care of everything. I don't trust her. With kids like her, Otto doesn't need enemies."

The Desmonds go visiting

Janet is at Rose's door. Rose suspects that Janet means to be visiting Joan or looking for Steve, because not many people knock on Rose's door and because Rose can see the Desmonds' Audi parked on Joan's driveway. But she lets Janet in anyway. She could use the company, and Joan doesn't want it. Rose knows this, because when Rose called after seeing the ambulance, Joan told her not to come over today, she is fine, that she needs to be left alone for a day or two, that's all. Yet she let Steve Desmond in....

Rose makes tea and puts home-made sugar cookies on one of her best plates, part of the set in the china cabinet that she uses only at Christmas, when she sets an especially festive table for three. Because Rose does set her table for three, routinely, though she's been living alone for decades. It helps her stay connected to reality, the reality of her past life when her husband and son were alive. When they were a family. (Rose also says, to the framed photographs she keeps by her bed, "Good morning, sweetheart! Good morning, son!" when she wakes up, and, when she turns out the light at night, "Time for sleep. See you tomorrow, my dears." She wouldn't be able to live if she didn't look at every feature of their faces twice a day, if their aspects were to fade from her memory over time.)

Rose chews on a cookie and listens to Janet talk about her son. "What will that boy do when Steve and I are gone?" Rose knows nothing about Brian's brain tumour; Janet has forgotten that she and Rose are not in the same circle, it seems to Rose, but she makes soothing sounds as if they are old friends and does her best not to react as if otherwise. She nods and brushes off the loose grains of sugar and crumbs that have fallen onto her lap.

When Janet stands up to leave after only a few minutes, Rose sees the chair she was sitting on is soiled. Oh well, thinks Rose, soda water will take that out. She wouldn't want to embarrass Janet by mentioning it. She has to raise her voice to tell Janet, who has left the front door open behind her, to come back anytime.

Word has gotten around very quickly this morning and Joan finds Steve Desmond on her doorstep. He is the first of the neighbours to come by. If he'd called first, Joan would have told him not to bother, but she decides to let him in. She'd rather not stand on the stoop chatting in public view right now.

"Joan, I'm sorry about Larry," Steve says. "Janet sends her condolences too, of course."

"Thanks." Joan has been drinking martinis all morning. "Can I get you something? Some juice, or maybe something stronger?"

"Sure," Steve nods. "Orange juice and vodka, if you've got it."

Joan mixes and hands him his drink and stares at him, waiting for the rest of what's coming.

"Tell me, Joan. You didn't poison him, did you? I mean, maybe you had your reasons. Or maybe he did something crazy, was that it? I'd bet you're the kind of woman a man could go crazy over."

Joan turns her back on Steve, runs the tap, half-fills a glass and drinks it down.

"I don't think this is an appropriate conversation to have right now, Steve." She pours another martini for herself. "But for the record, I'm not the killing kind, or I would have done it a long time ago. The worst I ever did to Larry was serve him his own urine in a wine glass and tell him it was Chardonnay."

Steve smiles, makes a show of sniffing his drink, then swallows half of it in one go. "Thing is, Joan, I finally figured out where I've met you before. I remember you." He finishes his drink. "So I get it, what Larry had over you." He hands her his glass for a refill.

"Do you now?" Joan empties her own glass.

"I do. I saw you there once, at that club in Chicago. You know the one I mean—where Bill Cosby and Warren Beatty used to hang out and play with the waitresses upstairs. I haven't told anyone, of course. Though a few people might like to know who the real Joan Palmer is."

"Perhaps they would. Gossip pretty much drives what passes for a social life around here. And speaking of gossip, perhaps people like your friends the Olivers and the Sommerfelds—perhaps they'd like to know about what really happened to you, a few years ago. You know, that little problem with your medical licence."

"I don't know what you mean, Joan."

"Yes, you do, Steve. The woman who died of AIDS, after catching it from her husband—your patient—because you never told him that he had it... remember them? The wife happened to be a friend of a friend of mine, so I know what happened. That's right. The professional discretion of your peers couldn't keep the story quiet after all."

Steve finishes his drink, reaches for the vodka bottle and pours another. "I did what I thought was right."

"Oh, I know, sweetheart. The man was already depressed, because of his heart condition, and you figured he never had sex with his ancient wife anyway, so you played God and kept his diagnosis from him. But they did have sex, and he gave HIV to her. And you got a real deal, didn't you? Getting to resign and calling it retirement, instead of going through a public hearing. You should be in jail, for what you did. Me—well, all you could really say about me, dear doctor, is that back in the day, I helped people to have some fun."

"Indeed." *Steve holds his empty glass an inch above the marble coffee table for a second or two, then drops it, making Joan blink involuntarily at the clatter.* "I'll just leave now."

"Please, see yourself out. I've got a lot to do. I'm sure you understand."

I am tired after reading as much background and current information about Upton that I can find on my computer. It's been three hours since I left Shelley downstairs. When I go back down, the TV is on in the living room; Otto must be watching CNN, waiting for his mid-afternoon pills. My god, I have been here too long if I've already memorized the routines of J.'s grandparents.

J. is with Otto. Each has a glass in hand, half-filled with a golden-coloured drink. But J. shouldn't be drinking at all, which he knows.

"What's this all about?" I ask, pointing to J.'s tumbler.

"We're just having a cocktail before dinner. Shelley says it helps whet Pop's appetite. Tell her, Pop."

"Whatever," I say. "I have an errand to do."

I should have expected this before now, I think on my

way up the stairs. I used to like drinking, myself—wine, mostly, and the occasional gin and tonic, when J. and I used to go out together, or when I'd listen to him play in a bar somewhere. As a student in university, I realized that I loved the feeling of being drunk, the openness it brought out in me; I'd become hyper-social, wanting to stay all night talking with people I'd just met, wanting to set up the next meeting so we could get together again and drink some more. I'd wake the next day feeling foolish, wanting to undo whatever I'd done the day before. I couldn't afford to spend very much on liquor, which is probably what saved me from trouble: I've always been on a tight budget, despite the scholarship money that paid my tuition and rent.

While I am getting my things together upstairs, I think about one night when I was over at J.'s place. His roommate had invited people in and supplied the booze, and all was well until it was gone, and they were too. J. came out of the bathroom at two in the morning and smelled like spearmint; I soon found out that he'd just finished a large bottle of Listerine using ginger ale as a mixer.

I'd forgotten about that incident, or else buried it so I didn't have to think about it. Those were the early days of our being together.

I take the box with J.'s gift in it and leave the house.

Janet is lost

Janet wanders toward Main Street, not noticing her seersucker capri pants are not fully zipped up. She wants to go to that shop that sells tablecloths from Provence. It will remind Steve of the trip they took to Paris for a medical meeting, then added on a few days to visit the place where Van Gogh painted. Janet loved his sunflowers so much! She could not do anything as distinctive herself, of course, in her own painting, but Vincent had certainly been an influence...

But where is that store? She sees buses parked in front of the theatre, and people are sardined on the sidewalks, three or four across and arm-in-arm, stopping her from going where she wants to go. She feels her heart beating too quickly, a tightening in her chest, making it hard to breathe. It is so hot out today! These strangers are taking all the air there is.

"This is my air! I live here!" she says in a firm, low voice to no one in particular.

"Lucky you!" a young girl says, laughing at her. The girl is not as young as Janet thinks; she is mid-forties, the age of Janet's own children. Janet thinks about Linda coming home for lunch from school; did she remember to put a sandwich out for her? Linda is in grade five now. No, don't be so stupid! She's in grade six.

Janet turns around and walks back down the street toward the water. She is looking far ahead into the distance, as if she is an automaton or in a hypnotized state. The tourists walking in the other direction must step on the boulevard grass to let her by, or she will bump into them. She finds a bench with a few inches of unoccupied space at one end. "Hello!" she says to the couple sitting beside her; they are watching the sail boats on the water.

"Hello!" the man and the woman say to Janet at the same time. "We're here to see Miss Julie.*"*

"I don't think I know her..."

Janet laughs because the other two are laughing. People are funny!

"We have to go, or we'll be late." They say goodbye and leave before Janet can ask them how she might find her way home.

Max's Fine Jewellery, which is tucked behind Main Street in a small building, is surrounded by parked cars; other cars are circling, looking for a spot, but inside I am the only customer. I wonder how Max stays in business, since the tourists don't seem to know about his shop. I suppose people like Shelley and her friends, people who live here, come to Max for all of their jewellery purchases.

A clerk appears from behind a curtain at the back and asks if I need help.

"I don't suppose you would take this back?" I ask. "It's engraved, but perhaps the words could be erased, or melted, or whatever? So the bracelet might be sold to someone else, I mean."

The door opens again, and street sounds flow into the room. The clerk does not lift her head, which is tilted towards the bracelet in her hands, but she raises her eyes to see who has arrived. I turn and see Janet Desmond standing in the centre of the store, arms loose at her side, palms facing out. Her mouth is hanging open and there are white crusts at the corners of her lips.

"Hello, Janet," I say. Janet smiles, then takes deliberate, wide steps to the counter. She rests both hands on the glass case.

"I don't know you, do I?" Janet says to the clerk.

"Yes, you do, Mrs. Desmond. I'm Tina. Max's wife." Tina speaks abruptly and does not smile. "You've bought many pieces here. Those rings on your right hand, for instance. How can I help you?"

"Then you know where my house is?"

Tina ignores Janet's question. "Are you looking for anything in particular today?"

I touch Janet's forearm. "I'm Sam. J. Sommerfeld's friend? You probably don't remember, but we met the other day, at Otto's house."

Something isn't right. Janet smells as though she hasn't bathed, and fine rivulets of sweat are streaming from her temples to her chin. Her foundation and face powder are melting, changing colour.

I remember Janet didn't know who J. was, the other day in Otto's kitchen, so she probably won't be able to place me at all. But she seems to trust me, as I take her hand and lead her to the door.

"We'll stop in at Shelley and Otto's," I say to Janet, "and they will call your husband to come get you."

"The bracelet?" Tina is holding it in the air, speaking to my back.

"I'll come back some other time," I say over her shoulder, knowing I won't. When Tina sends the invoice to our address in Toronto, as J. would have instructed, I will let it sit awhile before paying, if I pay it at all.

It's 8:45 p.m. I start my car and take the road out of town. I've been in Upton Bay for four days now, and I can navigate the streets pretty well on autopilot. I am always surprised at how easy it is to establish routines, those pathways that make a place feel familiar.

The peach stand, a few hundred metres on this side of Evil Maple's driveway, is closed when I get there; the last of the fruit must have been hauled away in baskets loaded onto the pallets that will be brought back when the vendors return in the morning. I know that many of the farmers around here used to grow peaches in vast orchards and that the soil and the weather was perfect for cultivating them. A canning factory employed half of a nearby town, and a jam-making company, the other. Now, there are only the small-scale growers who have a few trees and drive their fruit miles from their land to set up stands like this one.[24]

I stand behind the cheap, stained, and battered folding tables that are left here each night. I watch birds pass overhead, trained for generations to ignore the netted grapes growing below, and think about the words *cultivation* and *culture* and how opposite their meanings have become, despite the common root. I think about what it must feel like to work the land, to be deeply connected to the cycle of sunshine and heat and growth and harvest. I wonder what it is like to live out here in winter, when the temperature and the scenery aren't so easy to adapt to, when the tourists and winery owners take their money and disappear to better climes until spring. I close my eyes for a moment and breathe in the cooling night air.

Matias surprises me, arriving silently on foot at 9:05. We talk for only twenty-five minutes, because Matias needs to be back before 10:00 when the collector comes. If Matias is not there, he will be charged a fine for late payment, he says. I want to ask what he is paying the collector for, but first ask about his injured hand. He tells me that he knows men who spoke up when they were hurt and asked to see a doctor, and they were fired and sent back to Mexico. He can't let that happen to him.

---

24   They used to sell a full flat or two to women who still knew how to put them up for winter; but most people now buy only one or two baskets, which, emptied, they will use in the fall for storing handheld gardening tools, or to support an artificial wheat sheaf as part of a Thanksgiving centrepiece.

I had stopped at the pharmacy on my way and bought a bottle of hydrogen peroxide, some gauze, and a tube of ointment with a mild antibiotic in it. Better than nothing. I show Matias these items and he nods, holds up his hand.

"Are you a reporter?"

"No," I say. "But I am writing a tourism article for a friend of mine. I'm freelancing—do you know what I mean?"

"Freelance, *si*. Like me, a freelance farmer, on this place."

"Yes, I suppose that's what you are." I remove the fabric wrap around Matias's open wound and gag a little, then apologize. Matias clenches his teeth when the peroxide seeps into the festering cut, then begins to foam; it bubbles up from the wound each time I pour fresh drops on top of the flesh. When the sizzling slows down, Matias takes a clean paper towel and pats at his hand, while I put the ointment on a piece of gauze. He presses the dressing against his wound, then shakes his head at my offer of clean bandaging. From his pocket, he takes fabric ties made from a torn-up white T-shirt to wrap around his hand. How would he explain my bandages to Alberto?

I understand that I am a hazard to Matias. He will talk to me now, he says, but I must not use his name when I talk to other people, and I cannot talk to the owners at the vineyard or its shop clerks or restaurant staff.

"No one lives here want to be in fields, so they need us to come. Is good work, but hard too. In Mexico we take *siestas* when it gets too hot, but here, no. Small break only."

I ask about the 10:00 p.m. meeting, and Matias tells me about the agent he pays each week. "A percentage of wage, *si*," he answers when I ask about the arrangement.

Matias is forty-three years old and has worked here for seventeen years and has nothing to show for it. But the job is not nothing, not to his family. In Monterrey, they live better on what he sends than they did before.

"What do you do back home? Um—what's the word for work—*trabajo?*"

"Ah, my work is with *mi tio*, my uncle—we make boxes, *caj*óns, *por los muertos*," he says.

I nod that I understand. I remember the coffin stores next to cantinas and shoe stores on the streets of San Miguel. Life and death, out in the open, elemental. I ask if Matias's uncle is busier now because of the violence, all the killings I hear about in the news.

"Many more die now, *si*," he says, "but many no afford a coffin. They rent them for funerals, this is what the poor do." His uncle set one aside for Matias last year, he tells me, when he was kidnapped.

"You? Why"

"They think I come to Canada, I'm rich," he says. They didn't kill him because his wife gave them what was left of the money Matias had sent back to her the summer before.

I tell Matias that I pay everyone I interview, even if I do not use their name or their story in my articles. I take out my wallet and Matias seems uneasy, but I tell him I am well paid for my work, and he takes the forty dollars I press into his good hand. It's what I had in my purse, and only a fraction of what J. owed Max for a bracelet I don't need or want; but it is cash, and not so much as to arouse suspicion for Matias back in the bunk house.

"Wait," I say when Matias turns to leave. "Can I have your email address? In case I have more questions later?" I hand him my notepad and pen, and he tries to write legibly, but he is right-handed, and the bandage makes it difficult for him to write smoothly.

"Is espensive, the internet, so I go to the café to check email one time, maybe, for two weeks."

I nod, read what he has written down back to him; he corrects me, I make the change and thank him. With a wave, he refuses my offer to drive him back. "*Gracias,* Miss Sam," he says.

"*De nada,* Matias." I watch his white bandaged hand swinging back and forth at his side as he walks down the road, away from me.

FRIDAY

The photographer has bailed. The shoot wasn't worth his time, he told Nick, who will pull photos from websites to put into my article.

"But I have something else lined up for you, Sam. You're going to get an aerial view of the Upton Bay region, with my friend Faisal." Nick arranged the flight at the last minute—not for my sake, I bet; more likely it's to help Faisal promote his new business, flying tourists above the wine region when they've seen all there is to see on the ground.

When I go downstairs to tell J. about the change in plans, he is letting a woman my mother's age into the house at the front door.

"Hi, Aunt Elisabeth."

"Hello, J. You look like you're hung over."

"Nice to see you, too."

"I don't have much time. Where is Dad?"

Otto calls out from the living room, where he is watching a talk show on television. "Lisbeth! That you?"

"Hi, Dad." Elisabeth air-kisses her father's cheek, holding him away from her with her hands on his shoulders. "Dad, when was the last time you had a shower?"

"Jesus, Lizzy. Do you know how hard it is to get undressed and dressed again? Wait till you're old like me, you'll see." Then, "Do you watch this show? I love this guy Regis, he's such a riot!"

Elisabeth is at the window that looks out into the side yard and down to the waterfront. "You know, I'd forgotten how large this lot is."

"It's been a long time, no wonder you forgot."

Elisabeth pulls a brochure from her purse: Bayside Manor.

"Have a look, Dad. At this place you'll have a shower at least twice a week, more if you want, and they do your laundry and change your sheets and cook your meals too. It's not cheap but you can afford it."

"They have waiting lists for years, those places."

"They have an opening for a trial stay this weekend."

"And what do you think my wife would say about this idea of yours?"

"From what I can tell, she's getting tired out from all the upkeep. I'll be back to pick you up. We check in at two-thirty."

We all say nothing until the front door slams shut.

"Well, Sam, that was my aunt. Pop, you okay?"

Otto says he is willing to try the Manor for an overnight visit after all. Getting out of the house suits him fine, he says. He's angry at Shelley for calling Elisabeth to complain about doing laundry, and for calling the doctor about having a catheter put in. If Grete had lived, she would have cared for him, and he wouldn't have minded taking care of her as long as he could. "That was the vow, wasn't it? Till death do us part? Both times, I said it."

I go back upstairs, leaving J. to soothe his grandfather. Shelley calls to me from the master bedroom. She heard everything Elisabeth said, from up here. She is packing, putting clean underwear, socks, and pyjamas into a small duffel bag that she says Otto used to use when he took a change of clothes to the golf club.

"Why couldn't she call to tell me before she shows up here? She's never warmed to me, even after all these years, even though Grete has been dead for a long time," Shelley says. "I bet she hasn't told John about her idea to move Otto out. John will be against it, wait and see, because it will be expensive, and it will cut into the inheritance. Or what's left of it."

Irv lunches alone

Irv goes to the clubhouse restaurant at noon, orders a beer, and sits at a table looking out across the bay. The wind is perfect and there are several sailboats out there; Irv imagines crewing on one, though he has never operated a rudder or tiller and doesn't know what tacking means. He remembers the huge ship on which he and Rita arrived from England: the salty, fishy-smelling air, the feel of the breeze on his face as the vessel eased itself toward the dock in Halifax. He was excited, and in love; but that day he also couldn't help imagining being on the MS St. Louis headed for the shores of Cuba, then back north to Halifax, standing on deck and gripping the rail, hoping they'd all be saved.

He didn't tell Rita what he was thinking, then, because he didn't want her to think he was unhappy. And he didn't want to be unhappy, so he stopped himself from thinking about the St. Louis.

Faisal picks me up and we talk easily as we drive to the small airfield on the outskirts of town. He wears a badge with his name embroidered on his jump-suit, like he's an old-fashioned mechanic instead of a highly trained pilot.

We go inside the portable office that serves as the administrative base for private air traffic in the area. Faisal puts quarters into a pop machine and hands me a can of lukewarm Coke. He buys another one and drinks down half the can. I take a sip to be sociable.

Faisal has dark curly hair, deep olive skin, and a heavy five o'clock shadow that looks like it will need to be shaved again before the end of the day. He tells me that he grew up in Toronto but trained at a college in Sault Ste. Marie and got his licence there. "It was a very small-town kind of place," he tells Sam. "Mostly unfriendly Italians. And you couldn't find any spicy food at all."

"That doesn't surprise me. I'm from a place called Copper Cliff. We're not exactly known for our cuisine, in the North."

I am nervous about the flight and find myself talking nonstop as we take off and start climbing higher and higher.

"In high school, a friend of mine had cousins in Thunder Bay, and I stayed with them one summer while I worked at a place called Fred's Kitchen. I only lasted for a couple of weeks. I couldn't take it," I tell him.

"Fred was just so horrible to his wife. He would be charming and sweet and then he'd suddenly turn on Annie, yelling at her in front of customers if she dropped a fork or didn't retrieve something from the fridge fast enough. But Annie got mad at *me* when I left! I was shocked—I thought she'd be grateful that I'd told her husband how awful he was being. I've wondered since if I only made it worse for her."

"Nah, he was probably putting on a show, you know, to act the big man with you around," Faisal says. "A guy like that."

"Maybe," I say, but I don't think that's right.

"Annie taught me how to peel a boiled egg: you slam each end on the counter, then put it on its side and roll it back and forth, just once, and the shell peels off pretty much in one piece, held together by the skin. Every time I boil eggs, I think of Annie. Funny, the little things you remember about people."

By now the helicopter is at its full altitude. To me, looking down, the town looks larger than it felt while I was down there, inside it. Up in the air, the purpose of buildings has disappeared, and vehicles are just tiny moving objects, while people are not even visible. Individuality, with all its needs and wants, has evaporated. The green clumps of remaining forest, the yellowish-brown swaths of cultivated land, and the black tracts of parking lots look like they make up some kind of board game.

People with power and wealth must see everything this way; they must hold themselves at a higher altitude—high enough that they can't see the details of real life below. They must believe that they are floating above the world, that they are not connected to the multitude of lives carried on beneath them. That way, what happens beneath them, what happens to all those others, isn't their concern. Maybe that's how they keep going, holding themselves up there so they don't have to see the suffering.

That's the only explanation I have for the vintners putting dozens of men like Matias into small, airless huts on land that is worth millions of dollars. As if they are not human, as if they are livestock that happen to have hands to do the work. As if wealth is not built on the backs of those who lack.

I try to figure out where Matias's trailer might be, but there are so many vineyards visible from this far up that I become disoriented, confused about which area is which.

Then, during the descent, I watch everything reappear: colours and details of streets emerge; buildings take on unique characteristics; and roads become identifiable pathways. So many people are down there, too—thousands of spectators wandering around, thinking they have entered the simple past here, in this preserved, Victorian village, where all is well, all is well, all seems to be well.

Joan holds her ground

Otto is sitting in the Adirondack on the front porch waiting for his daughter to return when an unfamiliar car pulls into Joan's driveway across the street. Two men about John's age get out, one carrying a metal post and the other a rectangular board. Otto watches as one of them leans into the back seat and brings out a mallet; they both proceed to the middle of the front yard.

When the hammering is done, when the men get back in the car and drive away, Otto reads "FOR SALE—COMING SOON." The sign does not belong to Elliott Realty, which surprises him; everyone uses the Elliotts in this town.

The men are not realtors, but Palmers—Larry's sons, who have driven up from Florida to deal with their father's estate.[25] Larry's boys will sell privately to avoid the substantial commission fee; it's a seller's market.

When the locks on the doors are changed later that afternoon while Joan is asleep—she had forgotten to lock the door again, making it easy for the locksmith to do his job and give

---

25   Larry did not marry Joan, but he told her she could live in the house, if he died first, for as long as she liked; unfortunately for her, he did not specify as such in his will.

the new keys to the Palmers—Joan calls her lawyer and refuses to leave the house.

When I get back to the house, around 6:00 p.m., J. tells me Shelley has gone to bed.

"Aunt Elisabeth came back when she said she would, and Otto wouldn't say goodbye to Shell."

"Do you think he is going to like it there, at the retirement village?"

"No, but that doesn't matter, if my aunt wants him to stay. She has power of attorney, and she can always claim Otto isn't being taken care of at home. In his current mood, he wouldn't argue."

"This all seems kind of quick, don't you think? I mean, just the other day we were looking at photo albums together, and now Otto won't speak to his wife—"

"Welcome to my world, Sam. I told you my family was nuts. You should be happy you have a small one. No father, no aunts or uncles, and no money to fight over."

Rose visits her friend

Rose knows Joan likely started drinking and stopped eating as soon as Larry's body was carried out the door yesterday, and who could blame her, poor thing. Rose has made some date squares and a tuna casserole to take over this evening.

Rose has never been angry at Joan, no matter what people around here might say about her: that Joan uses Rose, that she isn't a real friend. Rose knows being needed is not the same as being used. There was a time when Rose was lonelier than she realized, until one night when the two women found themselves putting out their garbage at the same time and Joan stopped and said hello. "Oh, I'd forgotten how good it feels to be spoken to," Rose remembers thinking at the time. She'd been living alone for many years in her parents' old place after losing her husband and only child in that car accident.

Once, when Joan was in Rose's house, she noticed there were three places set at the table and a crucifix high on the wall. She made Rose laugh about that: "Nailed him up there yourself, did you?" It was gone the next time Joan popped over, but the two extra place settings were still there. Rose had lost her faith along with her family. She'd simply forgotten about the crucifix because she was short and didn't glance up that high in her own house.

"Oh, it's you!" Joan opens the door wider. "I'm glad you're not Steve Desmond. Or those sons of Larry, who put up that sign."

Rose smiles. "Certainly not! Let me put this food in your refrigerator."

"I could use some more ice while you're out there."

Rose is almost afraid to open the fridge, but it isn't bad: near-empty bottles of orange juice, tomato juice, and ginger ale, mostly. Joan's house looks worse inside than Rose expected it to, though: plates and glasses cover the counters, the tabletops—even the floor, in front of one of the sofas. She takes Joan some ice in the one clean bowl she can find in the kitchen, then puts on the rubber gloves she found under the sink and starts washing up.

"Leave it, Rose. I want to tell you something."

Rose doubts Joan will remember anything she might tell her, in the state she is in, but she sounds serious. So Rose sits down prepared to listen.

Joan shuts her eyes, and begins:

"I was married once, before Larry. His name was Phil, and he was into cars and I couldn't even drive. It didn't turn out well. What happened was, I fell in love with another man, and I told my husband. He said he didn't want me to stay, if that's how I felt, and he started screaming at me, and told me to get *out. So I did, I left and went to my lover's house, thinking Phil would cool off and I'd go back there to live with the kids and Phil would go stay with a buddy for a while, until he sorted things. But what Phil did was—"*

Had Joan fallen asleep? Her eyes were still closed, but she shook off Rose's hand when she touched her shoulder, and continued:

"*What he did was he put the kids in the back seat of the car and got in behind the wheel.*" Joan was speaking very quickly now as if she was trying to get her story over with. "*He wasn't answering the phone so a friend of ours went to the house and found them in the garage with the car running. He was a mechanic, I guess that's why he chose to do it that way.*"

"Oh my god, Joan!" Rose begins to cry and searches in her purse for Kleenex. "I didn't know, Joan, if I'd known—"

"What? What would you have done, Rose? What would be any different if I went around talking about it?"

Rose understands what Joan means. Rose moved to Upton Bay after the accident, and she'd never told Joan anything about it once they'd become friends. She blows her nose and speaks very softly. "What did you do then, Joan?"

After the funeral, Joan says, she left her lover and moved to Chicago, where she rented a clean, small bed-sit under the name Brenda Chisolm in a house run by a strict Catholic widow. The woman believed her when Joan said she was in the city temporarily, to help a cousin start up a restaurant business.

(In those days, whenever Joan stepped out, people on the street noticed. She carried herself with a model's poise, dressed in Dior and Chanel hand-offs—finds from Salvation Army shops—with her red hair in a French twist worn high on the back of her head. She wasn't beautiful, but she was striking. Shoes and purses were matched sets, the jewellery elegant and spare, and her legs long and shapely. She held her head at a

regal angle that made instant sense of her mild British accent. Her husband Phil always thought she was too good for him.)

The weeks went on, and the months, Joan says; she was numb but surviving, existing on what she made as a gentleman's escort. Sometimes she brought a man back to her room with her, for an hour or two. One evening, catching Joan on her way out, the landlady asked if the restaurant was doing well and Joan said, "What restaurant?" So the woman stayed up waiting for Joan that night, which was one of the nights she brought her client home with her. She found an eviction notice dangling on her doorknob the next morning.

"What did you do then?"

Joan goes on talking about her life, confessing it: she used her newfound connections and landed a job as hostess—they called her the Door Bunny—at the Playboy Club, which also rented her a room on site, in the Bunny dormitory on the third floor, for $50 a month. The men she seated at round tables covered in white linen were in big business or one of the "professions," many from out of town, and there were some celebrities, too, who posed for pictures they later signed for framing.

"Like who?"

Joan best remembers the faces of Shel Silverstein, Bill Cosby, Warren Beatty, and each of the Rolling Stones. Try as she might, she can't recall seeing Steve Desmond there; but there had been so many men....

There. She's told someone. Now there is no power to Steve's telling of it because Joan has claimed it for herself.

J. and I order a pizza for dinner; Shelley is sulking and won't eat. Later, while hunched over my laptop on the bed, writing my article, I hear more sirens. I look out the window and see red lights strobing the dark sky.

At about 10:00 p.m. I hear Shelley answer the phone. She comes into my room, in distress.

At about 9:00 p.m., she tells me, a neighbour of John's found him collapsed in his driveway and called an ambulance; John had had a major stroke, leaving him unable to speak clearly or to move his left leg or arm.

We wake J. to tell him about his father, and I drive them both to the city hospital.

We can't tell Otto until tomorrow morning because there is no phone in his guest suite at Bayside Manor.

The Desmonds come undone

In Upton Bay, Linda Desmond, Janet and Steve's daughter, visits her parents to tell them that Brian, her brother, has been admitted to a rehab facility outside of Toronto. The brain tumour did not, in fact exist, which Linda discovered when she was called as Brian's next of kin and spoke with the doctors while waiting for him to wake up from an opioid overdose. The cash cow he'd milked for years was finally dead—but not before most of her own inheritance had been wasted on her brother. Linda insists that Steve transfer funds to her, to cover the program costs for Brian's recovery, because she sure as hell isn't going to pay for it herself.

Once Steve agrees that he cannot care for Janet on his own anymore, Linda puts her parents' home on the market with the Elliotts and finds an apartment for her father to move into alone.

With Janet institutionalized—not in the smaller, closer city, where Otto is, but in Toronto, nearly two hours away—Linda is able to visit her mother once a week. After one visit, Janet hands Linda an envelope before she leaves: it is a birthday card, wishing her daughter "a very happy day, whenever it is!" At this point Linda is finally able to laugh, and she hugs her mother goodbye.

Meanwhile Steve, who soon thereafter chooses to become mute, answering to no one, signs the rental lease that Linda put in front of him. As soon as the house sells, Linda puts the proceeds into a trust, which will make payments for the apartment and for Janet's care automatically. Steve spends days watching his daughter clear out the contents of his house. She sorts thousands of objects into one of three piles, labelled Toss, Donate, Pack. Dozens of empty wine bottles, mouldy boxes of photographs, piles of tangled church-sale decorations, thirty tablecloths, seventy-seven recipe books, Brian's hockey sticks and skates and Linda's doll houses and Barbie collection, and medical textbooks—two of which had been under the legs at the head of the bed for ten years creating the fifteen-degree angle that helps Steve with acid reflux—are discarded. As are: curtains, flattened and yellow-stained pillows, five cocktail shakers, three scratched Teflon frying pans, bags of moth-holed woollen skirts and blazers that never made it to the Goodwill store, dust-topped cans of diced tomatoes and jars of olives, metal ice-cube trays, three dozen tumblers, two sets of plastic patio dishes, broken lamps, stained sheets, fifteen pairs of worn-out shoes, four tennis rackets, card decks, cribbage boards, one sixty-year-old mattress, board games in torn-and-taped-up cardboard boxes, Brian's crib, Janet's mother's furs, Linda's university transcripts, crammed filing cabinets, leaking tubes of oil paint, bottles of evaporated turpentine, hardened brushes, half-covered canvasses, blank thank-you notes, Christmas cards from friends and unseen relatives in the seventies, two boxes filled with video tapes and two broken VHS players, several broken television remotes, countless beaded evening bags, and one red rotary telephone.

Steve watches handy Sandy pull in and out of the driveway with his pick-up truck, morning until night, loading things in piles according to Linda's instructions, tallying his mileage and waste drop-off fees, and putting favoured items—a drill, end tables, costume jewellery, and the antique butcher block that reminds him of his own father—under a tarp in his garage, for the yard sale he will hold in the spring.

"Dad, you won't need those medical books anymore to elevate your head when you sleep. The bed I'm ordering for you raises up however high you want. And you'll have new sheets, too—my god, those sheets you and Mom used! I know no one saw them, other than you two, but still! And I'm getting a set of new dishes, just four of everything so the dirty plates won't pile up. Besides, you won't be having dinner parties by yourself, will you."

Only those items needed for Steve's new household will be packed and put onto the moving truck, the chain of meaning held throughout more than one lifetime of possession now broken for all time.

"It's just stuff, Dad," says Linda when she notices Steve standing in front of the house, watching Sandy drive away with another load.

Witnessing the dispersal of his belongings, all those objects and furnishings that had surrounded him and Janet for the past fifty-five years of marriage, Steve thinks, "Now I know what it's like to be dead."

SATURDAY

After seeing John in the hospital, J. and I stayed up much of the night talking about next steps. The end of our relationship came more easily than I could have foreseen, because I couldn't have imagined J.'s rapid change of heart and mind about his father, or about Upton Bay, or where he wanted to be.

J. has decided that he *can* stand his father, after all, now that John can't speak, and that he'll be better able to recover his own strength—J.'s, that is—living on the means of his family as opposed to my modest support.[26] So I leave Upton Bay for Toronto by myself.

On my way out of town, I drop J. off at John's home, a new-build three-thousand-square-foot bungalow in a development just off the road that leads to and from "Olde Towne" proper. At an ugly, concrete mini-mall built to serve the new subdivision, I see a bank with a drive-through window on the side of the building. *Really,* I thought, *these people can't even get out of their cars to get their hands on the cash?*

---

26 At Christmastime, J. will join a jazz trio that plays in the lobby of the waterfront hotel his grandfather used to own. He will make more in tips in one night than Sam does in a week after working for five years in the café.

I remembered having a conversation with J. about the fact that human beings are getting lazier and lazier: "We had to invent the gym to exercise our bodies, because we don't use our limbs and muscles enough to stay healthy," I recall saying to J., who rolled his eyes.

"Ah yes," he said then. "It all started with the electric pencil sharpener. What was wrong with whittling, for god's sake? Sure, you might have lost a finger or two, but at least you weren't lazy!" I smile at the memory.

I pass the peach stand where I met Matias with my ad hoc first-aid kit of hydrogen peroxide and antibiotic ointment. I glance at the winery on my way by, where Matias and his peers toil to produce the elegant bottles American tourists tuck away in their trunks, hoping they can get through customs without having to declare and pay duty tax on them.

The drive home seems much faster than the drive to Upton Bay had the week before. I spend most of the two hours in my head, thinking about what I learned of Otto's personality and sympathies, about J. and his shift in allegiance, and about Matias. I thought about J.'s reaction to Matias's story, and how it had upset me. The speed at which the antagonism between us had grown over the course of just a few days surprised me, as had J.'s sudden forgiveness of John. But in truth, I didn't really know J. very well before his hospitalization, and who he became while he lived with me was someone else entirely.

I am not sorry about any of it. I am glad I spent this week in Upton Bay, where I will never belong, and I am glad to be leaving it behind. I am leaving J. behind too, in a town where, apparently, he always did fit in.

Part II

SEPTEMBER

When not on shift at the café, I've spent most of my days since leaving Upton Bay tracking down government officials, asking for more information about Canada's temporary worker program and the rights of those who are brought to the country to work so hard, for so little. Today, after spending thirty minutes on hold, I informed the representative I finally spoke with that at least one employer near Upton Bay is charging workers ridiculous rents for one cot of six in a retrofitted camper with a hotplate and no ventilation, when that employer is legally required to provide workers with a reasonable place to live; that the workers I met are being required, illegally, to pay back their airfare to the employer on arrival, with interest, or have it deducted from their wages with a higher interest rate; and that "agents" are collecting commissions on the workers' income on a weekly basis.

I formally requested that the Ministry:

1. order a re-inspection of the premises;
2. conduct an audit of Evil Maple, requiring its receipts for airfares and wages paid—including any deductions; and

3. post the report online, with photographs of premises and financial documentation.

I know that the last is not likely to happen, that maybe none of it will, but asking for these things is what I can do, what Matias cannot.

The government employee became defensive, so I was reassuring: *No, this is not a threat. The government has the power to do the right thing, and that's all I'm asking. No, I am not with the media. Yes, I am a writer, of sorts.*

I will post an article about the situation on my own website, which I developed on a do-it-yourself, free platform after returning to Toronto last month. I will also contact an organization I found online that helps migrant workers by meeting them in the communities near the farms and vineyards where they work, hearing their stories, connecting them with resources, and supporting their efforts to stand up for their rights. I can do that much for Matias, at least.

John's shenanigans surface

Otto is now a permanent resident of Bayside Manor.

The day after John's stroke, Elisabeth told Shelley that Otto is gone for good; a week later, she told her that Otto will be filing for divorce.

Shelley will get half the value of the house, but now that the lot has been severed and the waterfront section sold to a developer—John had been busy, behind their back—the value of the house that has been her home for the past twenty-five years has decreased by almost fifty percent.

(Months from now, when Shelley's lawyer researches the paper trail and speaks to potential witnesses for the coercion case against Elisabeth and John, John's secretary will remember the day she saw John throw crumpled notes in the garbage can. "His behaviour was unusual that day," she will say, and her gut told her she should look; so she retrieved the paper in case it had to do with council business. It did not; it was personal information John had written under the heading "PP," about the property he would co-inherit with Elisabeth from his father. He had estimated how much it was worth and how much he could sell it for, were he and Elisabeth to divide the lot in half using the power of attorney their father had set up long ago, once Otto was installed in a home. "No, I didn't keep it," she'll tell the court; it was none of her business, that information. She will provide the council meeting minutes they ask to see, showing John's vote for rezoning his father's property at Lot 57, among other conflicts of interest.)

ANNUAL SUMMARY of COUNCILLORS' MOTIONS

UPTON BAY COUNCIL MINUTES

Page 2 of 14

Moved (John Sommerfeld) and seconded (Brenda Slipp): that Council approve the development of a contained subdivision next to the Three Cousins winery. Carried.

Moved (John Sommerfeld) and seconded (Jack Miller): that Council approve the severance of Lot no. 57 and the rezoning of the undeveloped portion

> with waterfrontage to permit construction of a three-story condominium building. Carried.
>
> **Moved** (John Sommerfeld) and seconded (Kirsten McCaw): that Council waive the historical-building requirements for the reconstruction of the buildings damaged by fire on Main Street. Carried.
>
> **Moved** (John Sommerfeld) and seconded (Joe Graham): that Council increase councillor salaries by 5%. Carried.
>
> **Moved** (John Sommerfeld) and seconded (Brenda Slipp): that Council move its services online in order to decrease administrative salary expenditures. Carried.
>
> **Moved** (John Sommerfeld) and seconded (Jared Moffatt): that Council sell the property currently housing Upton Bay's Public Library to MorTar Developments. Carried.

Elisabeth moved most of Otto and Shelley's cash from their joint account into a savings account she set up for herself and Otto, which Shelley finds out only when the bank machine on Main Street flashes an unfamiliar message across its screen: "Insufficient Funds." Even Shelley's credit card is in Otto's name, so she doesn't exist, financially speaking, from the bank's point of view.

OCTOBER

"Know your audience, Sam. Rule number one. Also rules number two and three and four."

"And the fifth?"

"Keep your day job."

"Maybe I just need to find another audience, Nick."

"You could look at it that way."

I was right about Nick's edits to my article. He reduced it to four brief, descriptive paragraphs, plus four photographs with these captions:

1. Ticketholders in front of the theatre on Main Street.
2. A popular bistro serves local specialties.
3. Visitors take a horse-and-carriage ride through streets filled with beautifully restored and maintained Victorian-era homes.
4. An aerial view of the many wineries surrounding Upton Bay.

Oh well, I think, at least I get the byline and a publication on my CV. Then I post an elongated piece about the town on my new blog:

PRIDE AND PRIVILEGE

Posted October 6, 2006, on
samarajohansen.ca

Upton Bay
Permanent population: 11,547.
Population including migrant workers (March through November): 21,371.
Average number of visitors each year (June through October): 2,150,000.
Average age of homeowners: 83 and dropping.

It is a town people admire, envy, covet.

Previous generations of settlers, long dead, have been born here or moved here when this was a working town, mostly small businesses serving the farming community.[27] Everyone, back then, knew where the doctor lived, and

---

27 A brief socio-agricultural history of the region: The first people to set up villages across the territory and also the first to farm it were the multi-tribed Iroquoian-language speaking people who called themselves Chonnonton ('people of the deer'); they were named the 'Neutral' Nation or Confederacy by the Jesuits, because they abstained from the conflict between Iroquois and Huron groups, and the Hurons called them the Attawandaron, i.e., their speech was different from their own. The Iroquois destroyed the Neutrals in the 1650s. The French, who claimed the land in the 17th century (profiting from the fur trade), were defeated by the British in the 18th century. Settlers from Britain and Empire Loyalists began to arrive and brought European farming methods with them; cultivation expanded to include animals, dairy, wheat, potatoes, corn. By the 1880s, the canning of vegetables become the dominant industries, until fruit growing took over in the 1950s. Winery development began in the 1970s. —SJ, retrieved from Encyclopedia Britannica, https://www.britannica.com/topic/Neutral, 10 October 2006.

the pharmacist, the dentist, the lawyers, and both bankers, too. The large, elegant homes belonging to these prominent residents were mid-nineteenth century and sat on tree-lined side streets, set well back from the windy waterfront. Children grew up and left for university, then moved away to begin married life in various cities; but in the 1970s, these well-off offspring came back. They took over their parents' properties and made application to the province, seeking Heritage Status for their childhood homes. The brass plaques declaring year of construction were positioned by doorbells to be visible to guests and passersby; they were polished regularly by groundskeepers who arrived in teams with rakes, lawnmowers, leaf blowers, and fresh mounds of mulch once or twice a week. Retirement meant a return home to live out one's years in leisure.

And when those adult children grew old, and their own children couldn't afford Upton Bay? Fortune still shone on the privileged. The real estate market was booming with career-oriented, dual-income "Toronto people," who began scouting out smaller houses near the water. They referred to them as "cottages," and used them as weekend retreats. "We're roughing it!" they'd joke to their friends, who would visit when they had tickets to the theatre. Later, many renovated and expanded the footprints of their houses as far as the town would allow, creating stately retirement abodes in keeping with Council's aesthetic, following rules established to preserve the look of Olde Towne proper. Proud of their place in the town, of their ability to put so much money into an oasis, many couples created a private refuge in which they were as sealed off from the unseemly as people living in a town can be.

(Funny, their use of that word, "refuge"—as if they were refugees. But for them, refuge meant distance, not safety. They already had safety and security, property and possession, and then some. They were hiding themselves from the ugliness of *other* people's lives, the struggles of lesser beings, the unsuccessful, the have-nots.)

But that transformation was decades ago, now. Since then, there have been other newcomers, investors and entrepreneurs who have again changed the landscape in its entirety. Brass plaques are still polished, but interiors are gutted. Vans of contractors line the streets from 7:00 a.m. day in, day out.; gone are the local businesses, replaced with microbreweries and retail chains selling imported leather goods, catering to the unending stream of tourists who arrive in buses and cars on day-trips to a quaint place that takes them back to a simpler time—a time when life was slower, quieter, prettier, and easier than it is for them now, with their mortgages and three-car garages and highly scheduled children and doggie daycares. These folks walk up and down the sidewalks, admiring the small-town architecture of old as if wandering around a film set.

According to the powers that be, this lifestyle envy, this voyeurism, is what keeps the place on life support. Because it was dying. Attracting new blood to Upton Bay has become a top priority for this town, but no one wants the small-scale elegance that defined last generation's luxury; large, modern, smart homes are essential. Growth is essential, everyone says, as if it is a law of nature; but what this town is growing is not for everyone: it's big real estate and big business. Farmland and protected green spaces in the area are disappearing faster than Arctic ice.

Some say the town has sold its soul. Others say that progress is the only way to maintain the semblance of its identity. The mayor claims, on an official website promoting the town's vision for the future, that Upton Bay provides a rich tapestry of historical, cultural, educational, and agricultural opportunities; that vineyards have replaced orchards in a time-honoured tradition of rotating crops; and that economic empowerment is the key to maintaining Upton Bay's status as a destination for visitors and a vibrant place to live for residents.

So, gone are the orchards, replaced by vineyards on which migrants from Mexico and Jamaica do the hard labour and are paid less than any Canadian would be, doing the same work—had there been any Canadians willing to do it, that is. What is missing from this picture are fair employment opportunities and housing for agricultural workers—reasonable living standards for the unempowered who work the land, those who provide the labour that creates the wealth for those modern-day "farmers" who grow "crops" and convert them all to wine.

Stay tuned for a post about the Ministry of Labour's response to my request for an inspection and audit of one such grape-growing landowner's operation....

NOVEMBER

Otto died earlier this month. J. called me and said that both he and John cried in public at the funeral, which was remarked upon by John's restaurant staff and by the town councillors who attended out of courtesy, for the most part, and not friendship.

J. forwarded a link to the official obituary:

> SOMMERFELD, Otto Jakob. It is with sadness that we announce the peaceful passing of our father and grandfather, with family by his side, on Saturday, November 12, 2006, at the age of 95. Predeceased by first wife Grete and brother Klaus. Loving father of Elisabeth (Jeffrey) Schubert and John Sommerfeld. Dear Opa/Pop of Jay Sommerfeld, Jeffrey Schubert Jr., and Cindy Schubert. Fondly remembered by extended family and friends across the Upton Bay region and in Kitchener. Otto was a prominent businessman and a successful investor until he retired and began his second career as a hotelier in Upton Bay. He served as a board member of Upton Credit Union for 28 years, as Chair of the Upton Historical Society for 10 years,

and on various committees of council, including Land Planning. A funeral service will be held at Bayside Mennonite Church on Tuesday, November 16, 2006. Cremation to follow.

No mention of Shelley, Otto's second and current wife of twenty-five years, divorce proceedings aside. Also missing, I notice, is mention of where Otto was born, when he came to Canada, and how he had made a new life here, starting over as a farm labourer.

I remember how Otto had spoken of that experience, about the humiliation he felt as a German immigrant being treated the same as a refugee. Perhaps he'd pre-drafted the content of the obit himself. Or perhaps Otto did have a past that was unmentionable? Maybe he'd had some sort of involvement in the German military he didn't disclose at his immigration screening in 1952, information which would have prevented him from obtaining citizenship.

I read an article not long ago about a retired businessman from Kitchener, around Otto's age, who'd had his citizenship revoked after an investigation prompted by the Simon Wiesenthal Centre. Oberlander, that was his name; he'd worked in the *Einsatzgruppen*, a Nazi squad that killed nearly 100,000 people, mostly Jewish, in occupied Russia. In his defense he claimed he was forced to work as a translator and to run errands, that he had nothing to do with the atrocities. That he'd had no choice. He appealed the deportation process started against him for lying about his wartime record during his 1953 immigration interview. His daughter, speaking to the press, said the government should leave an old man—especially one who had contributed to Canada's business community for decades—alone.[28] Perhaps he'd even been a friend of Otto's in Kitchener?

I start to wonder about the coincidence of Otto moving to the same area as Oberlander after the war. How did Otto represent himself at his own immigration interview? What did he say about his activities during the war—that he was serving his country, that he was following orders? Was he truly only a young man from a small farming village who had never met a Jewish person, who dug up potatoes and managed his father's dairy cattle before he was drafted? Or could he have been one of those Mennonite guards at Stutthof, for example?

What did Otto do? What did he know?

I go online to the *Deutsche Dienststelle*[29] website to see if I can find Wehrmacht records of Otto's service but, since I am not a relative, I am not even allowed to make an application for a search.

---

28 The case against Helmut Oberlander (b. 15 February 1924) began in 1994. The Federal Court determined that Oberlander had been part of the Ek 10a from 1941 to 1943, though it lacked evidence that he committed crimes against humanity directly or indirectly.

29 A database with personnel documents, listings, documents on military losses, and a register containing over eighteen million soldiers from World War II. Requests may be submitted for reports of one's ancestor's basic biographical information, including draft date, dog tag number, training units and units in the course of war, ranks, notes on injuries and captivity. Wait-time for report, if records exist: up to two years. www.dd-wast.de/en/assets.html

DECEMBER

I insisted on having time off this Christmas, which I've covered at the café for three years running, to spend the holidays with my mother in Copper Cliff. I've had my old room back during visits home ever since my grandmother died five years ago. My mother had moved Sigrid into the apartment for the last two years of her life. She never told me why she made that decision, even when I questioned whether it was the right thing to do, to keep Besta out of a hospital, especially when I knew they had never gotten along.

During the drive I think about the last time I had driven up, when my car's alternator died en route and I'd had to call the CAA to tow me to a garage in Parry Sound. My mother gave me money for Christmas that year, which helped me to pay off most of what I'd had to charge to my credit card to get the car going again.

I haven't been home in years, but everything looks the same: the wide streets with no sidewalks, old maples on front lawns of modest, wooden bungalows, with a pizza place and a Tim Hortons the only restaurants in town. The Stack—which made the town famous in its day, before the CN Tower was built, for being the tallest structure in the world—still stands, though it isn't functional anymore; it had been built to solve Copper Cliff's pollution problem, by pushing the smelter's poisons up so high in the air that the wind would blow it all someplace else, to become an issue for other people.

My mother must have been looking out her kitchen window as I parked in the lot behind the low-rise building, because she is waiting on the landing for me.

"Hey, Ma! How are you?"

"I'm so happy to see you! You're still driving that old car?"

"Well, it refuses to die. It has over two hundred thousand klicks on it, but Volkswagens can go over three."

"I hope it has a good heater, since you have a tarp for a roof. Come on, I'll make some tea to warm you up."

Mom looks heavier to me; she seems to have forgotten her golden rule, "If you can pinch an inch, lose it." Nonetheless, we nibble on the deep-fried *fattigmann* and the *pepperspisser* cookies she'd made a few days before my arrival as we catch up. There was the whole story of J. and the break-up to tell, and I told her about how the freelance assignment I'd taken from Nick didn't turn out as planned.

"I got sidetracked from the story when I found out what went on at the vineyards that I was supposed to be promoting. I met one of the foreign workers at a winery and he told me about the horrendous circumstances he and his friends were in. When I got home, I did some research about the situation and got involved with some people who'd organized, to push the government to take action." I open my laptop and show my mother my blog posts, which had been cited by the group and helped them to get the attention of local politicians.

"I'm so proud of you, honey."

"Thanks Ma. I want to do more writing like that, about issues under the surface. About things people don't know about, or don't want to know about."

She was smiling at me. "I always thought you should be a writer. You have more going for you than most people who pour coffee for a living."

"You can't live on words alone, Ma. Plus, I think you have to hit a certain age before you have anything to say. It took me this long to stumble onto a story—one I wasn't even supposed to be writing about."

"I have an idea for a project you could write about," she says, with a sheepish look on her face. "You could write about immigrants who came here after the war. You could tell your grandmother's story."

"Maybe," I say, stalling and trying to be polite. "She was hardly a typical immigrant, though." I pause and think of Besta. "She was a tough old broad."

"I can't blame her, really. She had a pretty hard life."

I stop licking sweetened whipped cream from the electric beaters left lying on the kitchen counter. "That's the first time I've heard you say anything like that about Besta. You used to tell me how cruel she could be to you. Like the time she hid in a neighbour's apartment when you were six, and you got home from school and were calling and calling for her, crying, but she wouldn't answer."

"That's true. She finally walked in and said, 'Surprise!' and laughed at the tear stains on my face. She was trying to toughen me up, she said."

"She was strict when she looked after me. Remember that time at the Lodge when I went for a bike ride to get away from her after she'd scolded me for something, and I took a bad fall? You stopped sending me to spend summers with her, after that."

"Yes, I did. But I've been feeling more sympathetic toward her lately. Maybe it's because I'm getting close to the age she was when her cancer was diagnosed."

"Ma, you're not feeling well?"

"I'm fine, Sam. I get checked every couple of years, don't worry. You should, too, when you get to be forty or so, by the way."

"Yeah, yeah. My doctor knows the family history. We'll be onto it."

"You know," she says, softly, "it wasn't until after my mother died that I was able to forgive her." Her voice trembled as if she were about to cry, which is not her nature. "I don't want that to happen between us, Sam."

"What are you talking about?" I put my hand on hers. "Why so sad? I have no grudges against you, Ma."

"Not now, maybe."

"I can't think of anything you could do that I wouldn't forgive, Ma."

"We'll see."

My mother and I always opened our gifts before going to sleep on Christmas Eve, in the Norwegian tradition.

This year, I give my mother:
– A velour bathrobe from Winners;
– Lilac-scented hand lotion from an Etsy vendor;
– *The Year of Magical Thinking* by Joan Didion;
– *On Beauty* by Zadie Smith (both books second-hand, but in excellent condition); and
– A book of stamps and a box of note cards and matching envelopes (my mom is a letter-writer, not an e-mailer).

My mother gives me:
– An Esso gift card for $50;
– modal-fiber pyjamas in periwinkle blue, with a cat appliqué on the top's pocket;
– A round, pewter key fob, engraved with my initials;
– An envelope with $100 cash for "fun money"; and
– A banker's box with a bright red ribbon tied around it.

The box contains loose sheets of paper with notes written in royal-blue ink, in my mother's hand, as well as a few cassettes.
"What's all this?"
"I have something to tell you. It won't be easy to hear. I learned something from my mother before she died, a terrible secret… It's been five years, and I still can't talk about it. But the guilt of keeping it from you is getting to be too much for me. I hope you'll forgive me."

I have no idea what she is talking about, but I tell her I will, of course I'll forgive her. I try not to look at the items in the box, but to look at her while she speaks so she will keep talking.

"It was shocking to learn what I did," she says. "So many things about my mother's life suddenly make sense now, but this secret has completely upended my understanding of who I am, and where I came from. I'm not even sure I want you to know," she laughs gently, "but I think I owe you the truth."

We've never spoken like this, my mother and me. What did she want me to do with the contents of the box, with the terrible family secret it held, whatever that turned out to be?

"Sam," she said, as if reading my mind. "You can do whatever you want with the information, as long as you don't get angry at me."

"Ma, how bad can it be?"

"It's bad. You know, I was always jealous of my friends, growing up, because they had aunts and uncles and cousins in their lives. And I felt badly for you, too, growing up as an only child of an only child. Just you, me, and my mother, for every holiday. But when I learned the truth, I was glad there was an ocean between me and my relatives."

Then she asks me to put the lid on the box and not to open it again until I get back to Toronto. "You can take my old tape recorder with you, too. Don't play any of the tapes here. I don't think I can stand to hear my mother telling her story a second time."

I promise my mother that I will tell her when I've started to read the notes and listen to the recordings of Besta's voice, so that she won't be wondering whether I know the secret yet or not.

"Try not to ask me anything until you've heard all the tapes. And don't forget what you said," my mother pleads.

"What did I say?"

"That you'll forgive me."

JANUARY

In the New Year, I call J. to wish him well. I tell him about my mother's gift, the archive of notes and tapes from her conversations with my grandmother. I was going to tell him there is a family secret in there that my mother has kept from me, but he doesn't seem interested; he is too eager to tell me about what's happened in his life in Upton Bay.

I've never heard him speak so fast, other than when he was on a high dose of steroids; he can't seem to get the story out fast enough.

"Dad sleeps most of the time and hasn't looked at any mail since he was discharged from hospital, right? I manage his accounts and bills online anyway, using his credit cards, so there isn't much mail. But one day in early December, a registered letter arrived addressed to John Sommerfeld, and I signed for it. My name being my father's initials has come in handy."

"And?"

"The letter was from an art dealer in New York. Inside it was a bank draft for a large amount of money—Sam, I'm talking over a million bucks—and a thumbnail photograph of a painting, the one I remembered hanging in

Otto's house, the one that Shelley and Otto said they didn't know where it had gone."

"What?!"

"It was a Schiele, an actual Schiele! It's called *The Small Town VI*, and it's a watercolour landscape of houses clustered together on a hill next to a river, in front of the road of a village. I guess I had great taste, even as a kid, huh?"

"Jesus, really? So your father sold it, and that's why Otto didn't want to say anything about its whereabouts! Shelley must have been told not to let on that John had taken it from the house."

"My father could have stolen it from Pop, that wouldn't surprise me. Anyway, the provenance information says that my great-great-uncle, Heinrich Lippert, had owned it in Berlin. Somehow it ended up in my grandmother Grete's hands after the war."

We hang up after a few minutes, but something bothers me about J.'s news. I decide to write to him.

Dear J.,

I keep thinking about that painting. Why would Grete's family send it to her in Canada? What other information was provided about the provenance of her uncle's painting?

Curious Sam

Dear Curious Sam,

Heinrich purchased it from a Berlin gallery owner, Karl Bucholz,[30] in 1941; this Bucholz acquired the painting from another dealer in Vienna, who had purchased it in 1940, from the original owner—a woman named Emma Finkelstein.

I've been following a few news stories about Jewish-owned artwork that was plundered before, during, and after the Second World War, including one in the *New York Times* about the provenance of Egon Schiele's *Portrait of Wally* and *Dead City III* and the legal battle that went on for decades to return them to the descendants of the rightful owner.[31] I know J. is not interested in history or artwork in any serious way, and I know his schoolboy prodding of Otto about his family's activities in Germany during the war were not based on any profound sense of guilt for the past, but more on his rebellious youthful nature.

Dear J.,
I'm not sure what to say. I'd congratulate you on

---

30 Karl Bucholz was a competitor of Alfred Flechtheim, a Jewish art dealer with galleries in Dusseldorf, Berlin, Frankfurt, Cologne, and Vienna. Flechtheim gave glamorous parties in his galleries that attracted movie stars, artists, and other members of the cultural elite. The Nazis confiscated Flechtheim's holdings, sold off his private collections, and "Aryanized" his galleries.

31 The *Wally* painting, on loan in 1997 to the Museum of Modern Art in New York from Austrian Schiele expert Dr. Rudolf Leopold Museum, was eventually repurchased by the widow of Dr. Leopold and, after legal fees, the proceeds were distributed to the heirs of the then-deceased original owner, Lea Bondi, from whom the painting had been stolen in 1938. legalresearchclub.ua.edu/blog/2020/01/27/the-united-states-of-america-v-portrait-of-wally/

your "winnings," but I am not sure they are really yours (or your father's) to keep. Don't you think you and/or the art dealer who sold it to your great uncle owe at least some of the proceeds to the original owner's family?—Sam

Dear Sam,

She sold the piece, it says so in the document, so why would there be a debt owed to her family?

Dear J.,

It is well known that any Jewish person selling art in the forties would have sold under great duress and for a fraction of market value. It is a question of morality and ethics. It's called restitution. It's becoming a big international issue.

Sam,

I doubt the sale to my great-great-uncle would have taken place if there were anything unethical about selling it. I'm not going to lie, the funds are a lifesaver. I'm playing in some local gigs, but you wouldn't believe how expensive it is to run my father's house and to pay for his care. His accounts were all but empty before this happened.

Take care of yourself.

This exchange with J. makes me wonder if I should report the existence of the Schiele painting to one of the organizations that promotes tracing ownership of art that had been taken or nominally purchased from Jewish people.[32] But what authority do I have? I'm neither a former owner of the work, nor related to the original owner of the painting that J. so fondly remembered hanging in his grandparents' home.

J. just emailed me again:

> *PS. Maybe you should find out what secrets your own family has about what your relatives were up to during the war....*

Last night I talked to Fern for a long time. Fern is a substitute elementary school teacher who thinks she can't start her life for real without a full-time position and—more importantly—without a partner. I thought she was joking when, soon after we met in university, she told me she'd been husband-hunting since she was about eight years old.

We've talked more often since I broke up with J., whom Fern never liked. When I told her about the Schiele painting and that I was wondering what I should do, she said to let it go, that it was none of my business.

"I'm surprised you'd say that. What about the descendants of Emma Finkelstein, the woman who owned the painting before the war?"

---

32 "The Commission for Looted Art in Europe (CLAE), established in 1999, is an international, expert and non-profit representative body which researches, identifies, and recovers looted property on behalf of families, communities, institutions and governments worldwide. It negotiates policies and procedures with governments and cultural institutions and promotes the identification of looted cultural property and the tracing of its rightful owners. It provides a Central Registry of Information on Looted Cultural Property 1933–1945 at www.lootedart.com to fulfil Washington Principle VI, which called for the creation of such a repository of information." www.lootedartcommission.com/Services

"If you were a journalist or something, maybe you could interview the gallery owner who bought the piece from J.'s father, find out if the gallerist checked out its provenance, and write an article about it. You could probably pitch that story to a major newspaper. But lots of Jewish heirs have lost court cases about art that was looted or sold under duress. And I doubt J. would tell you the name of the gallery, for starters. Do you think he'd want to give back the money?"

"Good point." Still, I was surprised that Fern didn't think I should pursue the issue someway. I didn't like the way I was feeling, like I was part of the deception, even though I knew I didn't have the authority or funds to take the case anywhere.

I'd told Fern previously about the archive box my mother gave me at Christmas; she asked me about that, and I confessed I've been avoiding it.

Then, Fern made her own confession to me: she was getting a nose job.

"Oh, come on! You can't be serious."

"I'm totally serious. I figure if I haven't adjusted to my profile by now, I never will."

I asked Fern if she could afford the surgery.

"My mother is giving me the money."

That did not surprise me. I recalled a conversation I'd had with Fern's mother when we were still students. I'd taken the subway up to Fern's home for dinner one Friday, as I often did. After dessert, when Fern went into her father's study to help him fix his printer, Fern's mother told me she was worried about her daughter—she feared she wasn't ever going to meet anyone. I was with Brad, in those days. I knew Fern was not happy about being single, so I thought she must have complained to her mother about being lonely.

"Oh, so you're concerned about her anxiety," I supposed, but Fern's mother laughed and shook her head. "No, no, no, it's not that. It's her *nose*. She's got my nose."

Fern has since gone on lots of first dates that she arranges through an online site called J-Date. She always finds something wrong with the guy, sometimes criticizing his weight, even though she is so self-conscious about her own. Sometimes she meets up with a date in the café when I'm working, so I can give my opinion, but it never matters—there is never a second date. "Why waste time," she says, "when you know it won't work?" She trusts her instincts, which is good, I guess.

Tonight, there is a middle-aged couple on their first date in the café. They've been talking for quite a while. The woman is wearing a knee-length tunic with capri tights, her lipstick a fresh pink; the man is in jeans and wears a T-shirt under a light cotton jacket.

"The puppy follows me all over the house, I'm always tripping over her!"

"Unconditional love, that's what it is."

"My friends think I'm crazy, but I've been a lot happier since I got her."

"That's not crazy. I feel the same about my cat."

"Ah, you're a cat person?"

"Not only, but I do love Mason. I called him that because when I got him, he was so tiny he could fit in a mason jar."

The woman takes her phone from her purse and shows the man a picture of her cat.

"Adorable," he says. "Here is Steven."

"I love human names for dogs! Wait, isn't your dog a girl?"

"Yeah, but I like the sound of male names for females. She's Stevie, most of the time."

"Right, like Stevie Nicks."

"Do you like Fleetwood Mac?"

And on it goes.

As I ring in customers' orders and make lattes and espressos, I watch the couple stick-handle safe topics, one after another, smiling at each other the whole time, and I wonder if either the man or the woman—both about fifty-ish—feel a spark, or anything, toward the other. If not, then I wonder if they'd want to spend time with each other anyway, if neutral might be better than lonely.

Maybe Fern will reach that stage at some point in her search. I don't see myself ever accepting neutral, but unlike Fern, I don't mind being alone, either. It might be in my blood, this feeling of being secure as a single woman. Of being okay with who I am. "It's not fair," Fern used to say when we were getting to know each other. "You don't care about guys, and yet you always have a boyfriend. I must come across as being desperate or something."

Fern was always heavily made up. "You don't need all those cosmetics. You're so pretty, just as you are," I used to tell her, but she thought the lipstick and mascara were necessary to attract male attention. Now she seems to think a smaller nose will do the trick. I think of the futuristic movie, *Brazil*, in which elderly women bleed from their continual plastic surgeries, and shudder.

FEBRUARY

Since I started transcribing the tapes my mother gave me at Christmas, I can think of little else. Her handwritten notes are barely legible, more a record of her own thinking process than anything that would add to the recorded conversations she made while my grandmother talked about her life in Norway. One page I found buried at the bottom of the pile was like an unsent letter; she might have used it to rehearse, to prepare for her confrontation with my grandmother:

> Mamma, I know you don't want to go to a nursing home or hospice care, but you know how we always fought when we lived together. We are very different, our personalities. But I will make promises to you on certain conditions:
> 1. You can live with me, until the end, as long as you make an effort not to criticize my housekeeping, my cooking, or how I raised Sam; and
> 2. I will take care of you, but you must do something for me in return. You have to tell me what happened in Norway, about what happened to

my father during the war, and why there has never been any contact with your relatives in Norway.

I call her to talk about this ultimatum, even though she asked me not to question her about anything until I had finished going through all the material. She starts off being opposed to any discussion with me, but I insist—just like she had insisted that Besta open up to her.

"You handed me a bomb-in-a-box, and now you won't talk to me?"

"Okay, okay, Sam. But I am nervous, so please, take it easy on me."

I wasn't sure how to respond to that request, so I ignored it and started asking questions.

"Why did knowing about your family history start mattering to you while Besta was dying?"

"All I can tell you, Sam, is that you live your whole life with your mother there, a phone call away, available to answer questions or fill in gaps in your memory. You take that for granted. But when Besta was diagnosed, I started to think about not having her consciousness there anymore, and about how that silence would feel absolute. I would have no access to stories about my grandparents or who my aunts, uncles, and cousins might be. I always knew there was something terrible she didn't want me to know, how could I not? She wouldn't speak about Norway or relatives whatsoever. Ever. I just accepted it, as kids do—it's all you know, period. There was a line drawn around our lives, in Sudbury, and our little family existed within that boundary."

"You always pushed me to leave, to learn about the world—but you never did."

"Well, I had you, and I was single, so I needed my mother's support. But all that silence, the severity of it—it shaped me, and it made me introverted and small. I felt like I had to hide from the world."

"You hid behind your mother's wall of secrecy?"

"In a way. It defined me. But when her cancer spread and the radiation and chemo were stopped, I kind of panicked. Except I knew the feeling was a signal to me, that this was my chance, if I could be courageous enough to take it. So I came up with the bargain I did. I would have felt guilty, not taking care of her, but honestly, I would have preferred it that way. The promises I made had to be contingent on me getting what I needed from her."

Besta fulfilled her end of the bargain with my mother, but in her own way, her own time. She gradually built up the story of how she came to be pregnant with my mother by filling in the details of the family genealogy, along with descriptions of the town where Besta's parents raised their family. When the truth was finally revealed, it was shocking, but slightly cushioned for my mom, I suppose, by the context. At least that's what I imagine Besta's intent was, unless she hoped she might die before she reached the point of having to reveal the truth; because my grandmother was nothing if not strategic, and self protective, for as long as I knew her.

In the few conversations I have with my mother after that initial phone call, I try to be objective, to act as if I were interviewing a stranger for an article. I try to avoid earthquaking my mother's emotions, choosing instead to poke and prod as with a garden edger at the hardened ground of her psychological being.

I will work on the project on the project well into the spring, distancing myself from my mom as I go along by turning her into a character in a drama. I will complete a draft of... of what? What is my project, exactly? It's dialogue, but not a play; it's partly imagined, but it's true. It's a story about my grandmother—I'm writing out Besta's autobiography, in a way; but I'm also telling the story of her best friend in Norway, during World War II—so it's also a historical narrative.

And what a narrative it is.

I am going to put it on my website, and maybe someone will find it and be interested in learning more about Samara—not me, but my Norwegian namesake: Samara Lidelsky.

MAY

**GENERATIONAL CONVERSATIONS:
A DRAMATIC DIALOGUE IN THREE ACTS**
by Samara Johansen
Posted May 7, 2007, on samarajohansen.ca

ACT I

[Two women, an elderly mother and her sixty-year-old daughter, are in a simple bedroom. The mother is lying under the covers in bed, her grey-white hair braided and coiled around her head; the daughter sits bedside her, on a chair.]

–So, you want to know everything, Gudrun? Everything? How much can you take? We'll see. We'll just have to see.

I will start at the beginning then. What I'm going to tell you, no one else knows. Anyone who knew, they are dead. Long dead. So now I can tell you.

And if you end up ashamed, well then… so be it. This you already know: I started a new tradition, and you followed in my footsteps—single mothers, one daughter each.

Okay. So now I'm going to tell you what you don't know, since you are forcing me: we are not the only ones. We are not such a tiny family, me and you and Samara. You have uncles, aunts, cousins.

Remember you wanted to know about your background when you studied history in school? When you learned about Norway being occupied in World War II? I was ashamed, and so, I lied to you....

[Old woman begins to cough, hardly able to catch her breath.]

—Mamma, it's okay, don't upset yourself. We can talk more later.

—No, not later. Listen now. Later might never come.

—Go on, then.

—So. I was born in a town called Faldskaus.

—*Like the stew?*

—No, not like the stew! That's *lapskaus*. You never could keep any Norwegian in your head, Gudrun. Town names were made up based on the geography of the area. *Fald* is Old Norse for "fall"; *skau* means "forest," or "woods." So, Faldskaus means "Fallen Woods," from when the trees there were cleared to build *stavkirkes* and whatever shelter they had in the 1400s.

Faldskaus is inland, maybe an hour from Stavanger. It was a fine place to grow up, small enough that we all knew each other. At school the children were grouped into one of just two rooms. We made good friends that way, it wasn't like being in bigger schools in the city, or like your school in Sudbury, Gudrun. We played outside all year round. It was the Depression, but we always had the best woolen sweaters and mittens and socks, no one minded the cold or the snow.

There was not a lot of money in those days. And so, most families had gardens and grew vegetables and kept chickens. We ate lots of potatoes, like the Irish. So by the time the war started, we were used to having very little. There were rations, not enough food—the Germans took most of it for themselves, for the soldiers and to send back to their own people.

The stores ran out of things—no yeast for bread, and even if you had rations for sugar and margarine, you couldn't get it most weeks. If someone in your family could fish in the lake, you wouldn't go hungry, and my brothers were good at fishing. But some young men, bored and restless, left to find work across the ocean; they went to cold places like Minnesota and North Dakota. Some went to Canada, a few to Sudbury, like the Finns. They liked cold places, too, it reminded them of home.

One of our original ancestors was known only as Lukas—no last name! But the named ones, the Johansens in Faldskaus, go back to around 1560. Except the family name then was Steindal, for the parcel of land my father's people claimed, at the base of some hills where the ground had lots of stones in it. *Dal* means valley.

–And stein means stone, I take it?

–Right. So, A Valley of Stones, that was our name, and our land. A poor choice for trying to grow anything, but they survived, and then later, they did well. And so, in time, the area became known as a fertile place. Cows and sheep were raised by farmers. The family name changed to Vasett then, maybe because *va* used to mean "wade," and *seter* means "mountain pasture."

And so, a few families started to live closer together, and everyone took the same last name to identify where they came from. Children were named as the daughter or son of the father who established a homestead—for example, Petersdatter, for girls, Peterssen, for boys and so on. My mother was Jensine Salomonsdatter. It was all relations, your name was for *who* you came from, not where.

–Sounds confusing. What would happen if a Peterssen married a Salomonsdatter, for instance?

–If her given name was Aasta, she would become Aasta Salomonsdatter Peterssen; if her husband's first name was Arne, their children would have the last name Arnesson or Arnesdatter. My mother became Jensine Salomonsdatter Olsen, because she married my father, Kjell Olsen. But just before I was born, the government forced people to choose one surname for each family that would be passed down the generations. Some went back to names of their town or village or farm, others chose one of the names of the ancestors. For us, Johansen was taken from my father's ancestors.

–His male ancestors.

–Well of course! The world's always been run by men, Gudrun.

–I know that, Mamma. Even though we're the ones who grow human beings inside our bodies.

–Sure. And men resent it.

–Mamma! I didn't know you were a feminist.

–Oof, Gudrun. For me it wasn't feminism, just life. Just survival.

—Seems to me you controlled your own story at least, Mamma. By keeping it to yourself. Remaining silent.

—*That* I learned from my father. There were times that he might have been right, to hide the truth. Not always, but at times. You will have to decide for yourself, after I tell it to you.

—Okay....

—First, get a pen, Gudrun. You can write a tree.

Family Tree

JOHANSEN FAMILY GENEALOGY

*recorded by GUDRUN JOHANSEN, b. 1944
(Sigridsdatter; father, undisclosed)
according to information provided by SIGRID, b. 1925,
conveyed during the months of Sigrid's convalescence
from surgery/dying:*

Lukas, b. ????, d. ????
Anders Steindal, b. 1581
Abraham Andersen Steindal, b. 1646
Anders Abrahamsen Vasaeter, b.1690
Johannes Andersen Vasset, b.1775
Nils Johansen Vasset, b. 1797
Salomon Johansen Nilsen Vasset, b. 1832
Ola Johansen Vasset, b. 1866
Kjell Johansen Olsen, b. 1901 m. Jensine Salomonsdatter, b. 1903

Sigrid Johansen, b. 1925; Helmer Johansen, b. 1923; Per Johansen, b. 1924.

Gudrun Johansen, b. 1944

Samara Johansen, b. 1974

—So. My parents had three children: Helmer, Per, and me, the youngest. Father was called Kjell, he was a teacher. My mother was named Jensine. A typical Norwegian housewife: she baked, kept house, did our laundry, shopped in town, and fed everyone. She was very outgoing and talked all the time to other women. She had lots of friends. But she was very strict with us. The wooden spoon was not only for stirring the porridge or mixing the dough.

—I appreciate hearing about my grandparents, Mamma, but can't you start later in the story, like, around the time you met my father—

—Listen to me Gudrun. I have to tell you everything. Everything! So it will make sense!

—Okay, okay. Go on.

—Mamma was happy her boys were too young to be soldiers in 1940, when Germany invaded us. Helmer was not quite eighteen and Per a year less. The Germans would have forced them to join its army later, when they were losing so many of their own, but the Resistance blew up the Norwegian military files first, with all the records of names and ages and addresses!

—That's great!

—*Ja*. And so, eventually my brothers married and had children: Anna, Solveig, Endre, Margrete, and Birte. You can add them to your tree. Your cousins. My mother—

—Slow down, Mamma! You're skipping the entire war?

—You'll understand later. Just let me talk while I have the energy, please! So my mother wrote to me, it was a one-way conversation. I was forbidden to contact my brothers. I didn't want to write to them anyhow, not at first. I was still hurt and on my own.

—You had me.

—*Ja*, but you were a baby still.

—There's so much we're rushing through here! Anyway, we got to Canada how?

—This man my father knew in Ontario, who said I should come to Canada, he told the officials he was going to marry me. He'd been living in Sudbury for many years, working for the mining company. He had a hard, lonely life—and every time I talked with him, which wasn't often, I cried to hear him speaking Norwegian. He was a bachelor, a nice old man who helped us when we first came. We didn't marry, he got sick from the work. He died before you were old enough to remember.

1947 Passenger List on ship Sigrid and Gudrun travelled on to Canada

1947
Passenger Lists and Border Entries – Nominal Indexes

```
Given Name(s):    SIGRID
Surname:          JOHANSEN
Age:              20
Gender:           F
Nationality:      Nor
Ship:             STAVANGERFJORD
Port of Arrival:  Halifax Nova Scotia
Date of Arrival:  1947-07-26
Year of Arrival:  1947
Volume Number:    12
Page Number:      810
Series:           C-1-c
Microfilm Reel
Number:           T-61482
Reference:        RG 76
Item Number:      2652413
```

1947

Passenger Lists and Border Entries – Nominal Indexes

```
Given Name(s):      GUDRUN
Surname:            JOHANSEN
Age:                2
Gender:             F
Nationality:        Nor
Ship:               STAVANGERFJORD
Port of Arrival:    Halifax, Nova Scotia
Date of Arrival:    1947-07-26
Year of Arrival:    1947
Volume Number:      12
Page Number:        810
Series:             C-1-c
Microfilm Reel
Number:             T-61482
Reference:          RG 76
Item Number:        2652414
```

—Such a journey—on the boat, we shared a third-class berth with three other women. I cried the whole way, three days or more. Not you—you were a curious child, you were interested in everything, the boat, the train from Halifax to Montreal, the bus to Sudbury. You walked, holding my hand—you were only two and a half years old. I carried our suitcase, it was lighter than you were, but still I had blisters.

—I have no memory of the trip.

—That's best, it was not easy. There's a reason no one can remember anything before they are maybe four years old. I will go back to when I was a young child, about five years old, to tell this story to you.

—You've never talked about your childhood before, Mamma.

—Well now I will, so listen.

I met Samara Lidelsky when we were little girls. Sammi, I called her. Sweet Sammi.

The Lidelskys were from Russia. They came because Norway was a safe and peaceful place, no pogroms against Jews, and they lived in Oslo for many years. But there were other furniture makers there, and so Moritz moved his wife Rebekka and their children and his old father to Faldskaus, for the sake of their future.

Ours was a good town for the Lidelsky family to settle in, and the land was cheaper than in Stavanger. Moritz could buy enough to build a factory to make his fine oak furniture. No birch or pine for Moritz! The Faldskaus Mill produced the wood he needed, so he didn't have to transport it far. The whole town was grateful to Moritz, jobs were hard to find in those days, with the Depression starting, and Moritz had connections to markets in Germany that still wanted his goods. Without Moritz Lidelsky and his factory, our town would have had it much harder. People forgot about that soon enough, though—

—What do you mean?

—I'll get to that. You wanted me to tell you about the war, didn't you? So stop interrupting when I'm talking!

It was a very foggy day when the Germans landed. A day we could never forget. We could hear the fighting in Stavanger here in town: explosions, smoke from fires rising up in the air.... We saw a few German planes, with black crosses. Some houses not far away were bombed. Our windows were rattling!

We went into the root cellar then. Down the steep ladder, under the trap door in the kitchen floor. You could smell the earth when it was lifted. You couldn't stand up, down there. We sat on the bins of potatoes and turnips and carrots, whatever was left from the winter staples Mamma had put away. That was the last year we had so much food for a long time, we should have appreciated it more. I shudder now, thinking of that cellar with no light, and it was so cold, so cold.

We climbed back up after a couple of hours. And then we could hear the trucks and tanks going by on the road about a half kilometre away from our home, on their way from Stavanger to Kristiansand and on to Oslo. We huddled together in the kitchen, and we did not turn on any lights when the sun set, either. We were riveted to that window. I asked out loud if we should pack our bags and go to our camp, but no one answered me.

I remember eating plain bread without butter for dinner—we just passed the loaf around, tearing off pieces and chewing silently together. That is one of the last memories I have of our family being together, without conflict between us....

Oof, pass me that glass—*tusen taks*. I'm so thirsty, my throat is tired.

—Do you want to stop?

—No, I have to keep going or I might not be able to finish.

[The old woman takes small sips of water, a little at a time, as if it is painful for her to swallow.]

So. The Germans, they liked to march. All of them in the town, there were probably two hundred—imagine that, in a tiny town like Faldskaus! They requisitioned farmhouses, they just moved in. Some families had to live in their kitchens, the soldiers had the bedrooms. They took over the town buildings, even the school eventually, when more soldiers started arriving. They put cots in the school in the last couple of years. By then we had to have classes in different houses. Father had classes in our home, the other grades had classes in another place. This was after the teachers' resistance, when we were allowed to go back to school.

–What about the teachers' resistance—what did they do?

–The Germans, they were forcing teachers to change the curriculum. It was the same in all of Norway, the *pensum*—we took math, Norwegian, history, geography, nature studies, religion, drawing, and singing. I was very good at history, I won first prize, did I tell you?

–Many times, Mamma. Tell me about the teachers now.

–Well, they didn't want to change the *pensum*, to Nazify it. Quisling[33] and the Germans, they wanted to change what was taught. But the teachers won that fight. One thing the government did win: they

---

33   Vidkun Quisling was a Norwegian politician who started the fascist party *Nasjonal Samling* in 1933. The Nazis appointed him to co-lead the country's state administration (with Josef Terboven as the *Reichskommisar*) during the German Occupation, then made him the equivalent of Prime Minister. His surname became synonymous with the word "traitor" after the war. He was tried and executed by the Norwegian state in October 1945. —SJ

stopped us from singing our national anthem at school, "*Ja, Vi Elsker Dette Landet*" — "Yes, We Love This Land." We could be arrested if we sang that.

–Arrested?

–*Ja!* I read things in the newspapers Father brought home. All about Quisling's vision. He wanted to be Norway's Hitler! That's who he was following in the thirties, and he had plenty of Norwegians on his side.

And so, in Faldskaus, the official persecution of the Lidelskys got worse gradually, over time; but unofficially, it got worse almost as soon as the Germans came.[34] It was as if they gave people permission to express the hate that had been simmering. People you thought you knew, holding such poison in.

–Were there many antisemites in Norway before the Occupation?

–*Ja.* Even in our little town, where the Lidelskys were the only Jews, hatred was brewing. Maybe the factory's success made some people resent Moritz, even though he gave jobs to so many. Or maybe it was infectious. Maybe when people read what was happening in Oslo and Stavanger, they decided to take advantage of that mood to hurt those

---

34 April 9, 1940: Norway is invaded by German forces. May 11, 1940: The German SS issue an order to police to confiscate all radios belonging to Jews. The police are assisted by the national telegraph service, the issuer of radio licences, which provided accurate and up-to-date lists of radio owners all over the country, from which Jewish names were extracted. Norwegian census data provided by government administrators was from 1930 and out of date, but the census did include questions about religion and specifically asked about membership in Jewish communities, answers to which became useful for cross-referencing names on population registers and on the telegraph lists to confirm the cultural identity of Jewish radio owners. —SJ

under attack, maybe they liked to feel powerful for a change—who knows.

–What happened to the Lidelskys?

–Oof, such a sad story. So, one morning at school, Sammi found a note on her desk. I watched her open it and read it, and then she folded it back up and tucked her hair behind her ear, as if she was thinking about what to do. "What is it, Sammi?" I asked, but she put the note in her pocket without showing me and played with her thick brown hair, braiding it and unbraiding it, while we waited for class to start. She wouldn't say a word.

I finally convinced her to show it to me when we walked home together, when we were alone. It said, "We don't want Jews here!"

I could guess which boy wrote it, I recognized his writing from seeing his homework passed back to him, but Sammi begged me not to tell my father. Papa was our teacher. He taught the older children, so we were in his class. Sometimes I wondered if anything would have been different if I'd shown it to Papa. But later, I realized that that was like wondering what would have happened if Papa had been a different person.

–Did your parents give you advice about how to behave, once the Germans came to Faldskaus?

–Well, for one, they said we couldn't wear the paper clip.

–What paper clip?

–People made it into a symbol of resistance. The Germans made it illegal, but lots of people wore it anyway. And my father told me to be polite, to speak only if spoken to—that that was all I had to do, to stay out of trouble with the Germans. Not to help them and to be aloof.

The Germans hated that, and they made up a law that it was illegal to make a face or turn away if one of them walked past you or sat next to you on a bus in the cities. Imagine that! Trying to force people to like you, like schoolyard bullies.

I need some sleep now, Gudrun.

[The daughter pulls a quilt up to her mother's shoulders, brushes hair from her face. She leaves and comes back in the morning, when she hears her mother's voice. When Gudrun first comes into the room, she puts a small tape recorder on the bedside table behind a lamp and a box of Kleenex, where her mother cannot see it.]

Oh, the dolls, Gudrun!

–Morning, Mamma. You're smiling—you must have had a happy dream.

–*Ja,* I was dreaming about Sammi. All this talk is starting to bring her back to me.

–What were you saying about dolls just now?

–That Sammi, she had many fine dolls with heads made of porcelain, their faces painted pale beige with rosy lips and blue eyes, and cloth arms and legs with hands and feet made from china. I can still see their pretty, polished faces.[35] We played with them when we were younger for hours in her room. We made

---

35 An Asset Box belonging to Samara Lidelsky was held in the offices of the Norwegian government for decades. Inside the box was a list of the porcelain dolls that Samara had collected (gifts from her father, imported from Germany). The actual dolls had been taken by the police, after the Lidelsky house had been emptied of its occupants, and the dolls were distributed to their own children and grandchildren at Christmas.

up families with lots of girls who shared their clothes with each other. Sometimes we made fun with her grandfather, when he took his naps in the afternoon. He had a very long beard, and we would use a soft-bristle brush and then braid it until we couldn't hold in our giggles and he'd wake up. He never got mad though, he just smiled and touched the braid like it was something he'd asked for. In the summer we played hopscotch and hide and seek in the woods behind my house.

Her brother Leo was four or five years older than us, and he played violin. He took after his mother, with her thick, wavy hair and lively brown eyes. So handsome, a very handsome boy. He and Samara were close. I think I might have had a little crush on Leo. He had a girlfriend who wasn't Jewish, and his parents were very upset about that. But he was young, they thought he would have his fun and then later he would settle down, maybe with the daughter of Moritz's friend Rabinowitz—I think her name was Edith[36]—or someone like her.

Anyway, Sammi and I grew up together, like sisters. She didn't like my brothers, we had that in common too, so she didn't come into our house, but I

---

36 Moritz Moses Rabinowitz was a secular Jewish businessman who settled in Norway in 1909 and opened a clothing store in Haugesund, and he later opened stores in Stavanger and other locations. He made many contributions to the economic and cultural life of these areas. He fought antisemitism with lawsuits against national newspapers and he published anti-Nazi opinion pieces in the late 1920s through 1939. He was chased by the Gestapo from April 1940 until February 1941, when he was jailed in Stavanger, moved to Oslo, and deported to Stettin on May 22, 1941. He died in the Sachsenhausen concentration camp on February 27, 1941. None of his family survived the Holocaust. —SJ

liked going to hers. They had a piano and there was always music playing on the radio or Grieg records on the gramophone. Rebekka was a piano teacher and a few local children came to their house for lessons, so I wasn't allowed to visit then. I wanted to take lessons, too, but my parents said they couldn't afford to pay for them. Rebekka taught me a little bit anyway.

My mother's older brother Tore was a classical singer with a very loud voice. Once or twice a year he would come for dinner to brag about his latest invitations to sing, and during the Occupation he would talk about how much he admired Quisling. Mamma and Papa seemed to be afraid of Onkel Tore. After the war he made many records and performed all over Norway, but before the war, he was already famous in Stavanger. And Rebekka sometimes played piano there, at the downtown theatre when movies were shown, and Tore loved movies, so I knew he would have seen her. She was so beautiful, everyone knew who Rebekka was.

And so, I told him she was my best friend's mother, because I was proud of her. When I asked if he had ever met her, he shook his head and said he was disgusted that I would suggest such a thing. My mother said he only meant that she was married and because he was single, he must have thought I was suggesting something improper, which was ridiculous. He was one relative I was never sorry to have no ties with, famous or not. He had a different last name than us, so you can forget about him, too. Don't put him on the tree.

–Okay... but what about your brothers? What did they do?

—They studied at the gymnasium[37] and both got jobs at NSG[38] before the war started. After it was over, Per was made a manager and Helmer an electrical engineer.

Before I got pregnant with you, Gudrun, I was going to study to be a dietitian. You used to laugh at me for taking the job as cook at the Finnish Nursing Home, but I had more in me than you knew. I could do more than clean houses. I could have done more.

When I was at the Lidelskys' place I would talk with their cook, and she taught me some of the recipes the family liked. I learned how to make *matzoh*!

—I remember eating that, Mamma.

—Potato latkes, brisket—I tried making some of those dishes when we went to our camp in the mountains—the only time Mamma let me do any cooking was at the camp. Samara came with us many weekends when we went there, but she wanted to eat Norwegian-style meals, not the food she had at her home. Papa caught fish in the lake and Mamma fried it with onions after cutting the head off. I could never eat fish with the head still on—even seeing the tail bothered me. Helmer told Mamma I didn't deserve dinner if I was going to act like such a baby, because I pushed my plate away if she forgot to cut the tail off on my serving. Helmer would get two dinners then because I would leave the table in a sulk.

—Did Sammi's brother Leo know Helmer and Per?

—*Ja,* but both my brothers were jealous of my friendship with Sammi. Especially Per. Because it

---

37 Gymnasium is the term used for the academic (vs vocational) stream of Norway's secondary education system. —SJ

38 Norwegian State Gasoline company. —SJ

took me from his reach, probably, more than before. Per would pin me against the wall in the hallway upstairs and he would put his hand up under my dress, he would touch me *down there*. I bit my tongue so hard it split.

—That crack in your tongue you used to scare me with when I was little? You told me it was because you lied once, and your tongue split in two!

—He told me he would hurt me *down there*, if I told anyone what he did to me. He said Mamma would never believe me anyhow, and I believed him. He was her favourite.

—Mamma, that is horrible, what happened to you—

—Listen, Gudrun, you don't know the things that happened to girls all the time in those days. Not just me. I had a terrible brother, but there was worse, I found that out later. Are you going to listen to me or keep interrupting?

—Go on, Mamma.

—Sammi's brother, now—ah, Leo. He was the best-looking boy in Faldskaus. Helmer was jealous of *that*. So, Helmer didn't like Sammi being my friend either.

I've carried a lot of hatred for my brothers all these years, but at least they didn't look down on the Lidelskys because of their Jewishness. If our father hadn't been educated and the kind of person who encouraged quiet behaviour, they could have turned out just like my classmates, the ones who joined the *Hirden*[39] so they'd feel like big men, superior people.

---

39 Similar to the Hitler Youth, an organization of the Norwegian Nasjonal Samling party. —SJ

Our family was not religious. We only went to church on Sundays, to be like everyone else. The *stavkirke* was built in the thirteenth century of wood, and it was dark inside and out, and its carvings of serpents and dragons were frightening to me when I was small. When I got older it seemed strange to me that people in our town accepted whatever fairy tale was going—dragons, angels, whatever. Once we came to Canada, I stopped with that church business, you know that.

—I know, I was teased by my classmates for being a heathen.

—Those church people were not so nice to us. Back home, they were no better. Oh, some of them were, like that minister in Sandnes who saved two Jewish boys, eight and ten years old. I found out about that after the war. He got them to England on a private fishing boat, but he was picked up and shipped off to a camp and died there. Maybe he was killed. Anyway, he didn't come home again.

And so, the Lidelskys had no synagogue to go to in our town, Oslo's was the closest, but the family wasn't religious either, so maybe it didn't matter too much to them. Except they would travel to Stavanger for their high holidays to socialize, to visit people they knew in the Jewish community there. I was jealous when my best friend got to go to the city without me. I used to go with them, when we were little; Rebekka took us in Moritz's car to go shopping for good clothes for Sammi. She would have bought me a new dress too, but my mother forbade it after the first time. "What are we, charity cases?" she shouted at me. She was a little bit jealous of Rebekka, for the clothes she had, I think.

Gudrun, are you still there?

—Yes Mamma, I'm right beside you. Here, take my hand.

—I wanted to hear your voice. Oh *ja,* I was lonely in Canada for a long time. It must have been lonely for the Lidelskys in Faldskaus, too, but I didn't think about that then. Whenever I spent time in their house, the family was so lively and so happy! Samara said I was the best friend she'd ever had. But in 1939 when she turned fourteen, she started to talk about this boy she'd met in Stavanger, Hermann Goldstein, the son of her parents' friends. I think they were matchmaking for them, there were no Jewish boys in Faldskaus. She would have to marry a Jew, she said, and lucky for her he was very good looking and funny and intelligent.

I knew all the boys in my class and none of them were interesting, believe me. They were either stupid or bullies. Besides, none of them wanted a girl who wanted to study after high school to become anything but a housewife at eighteen. I was going to be a dietitian, did you know that?

—You told me Mamma.

—I knew three older boys who joined the *Hird,* they became guards at a camp. Before they left, one of them knocked on our door one day with a clipboard. He took down our names and our ages, as if he didn't know us, and asked us questions about our "activities." Were we involved in the underground? Did we know anyone who was? They wanted people to spy on each other! Like they do in Russia!

After the war I heard stories about what happened at the camp where those boys worked, the things they did. They really believed they were somebody, they were even bragging about their jobs when they came home. It made them feel important to hold people's lives in their hands. Hands that held guns they used like toys, because killing was a game they were allowed to play. Worse than the Germans, I heard. These were the boys I grew up with in our nice quiet town! After the war they fell back to their real places in life, but lower than before. Still, they thought they were better than me, they would spit at me in the street! And… and…

[Old woman starts sobbing and coughing.]

–Shhh, shhhhh, it's okay Mamma, it's okay, you weren't like them. It's okay, here—take your night pills. We'll talk more tomorrow.

–Okay, that's fine. But wait, what are you writing on those papers?

–I am only making notes, so I can think about things later. I can't write as fast as you talk. I won't put everything down, just words that mean something to me.

[The daughter turns off the tape recorder and the lamp before she leaves the room.]

ACT II

[Morning. The daughter brings a bowl of soup into the old woman's room with her and gently shakes her mother's shoulder to wake her.]

–Here, Mamma, eat a little broth for me.
–You're so quiet I didn't hear you come in. You have a soft voice, Gudrun. My father had a calm, soft

voice, too. I think a person's voice carries their soul. As soon as you hear someone's voice, they are standing beside you, even if you are only talking on the phone. What was I talking about before, Gudrun?

—You were telling me about being in school last night, Mamma. About the boys that you didn't like…

—*Ja, ja,* and school. The Germans said we had to be taught Nazi values, Nazi philosophy, Nazi everything. There was a new union the teachers had to join, but most teachers in Norway refused and schools were closed. To save face, Quisling had many teachers arrested and sent half of them to a concentration camp in Kirkenes, the far north, for not cooperating. They went to Grini, the concentration camp, first.

—Did your father go there?

—My father, no. He agreed to sign the papers to join the union.

—He what?

—He was not a Nazi, Gudrun, but he was afraid. His brother, my Uncle Sigvard, was already in Grini for listening to the BBC. It was illegal, but people did it anyway, so they forced everyone to turn their radios in, after a couple of years. Then Uncle Sigvard got one smuggled in on a fishing boat. He was the mayor of Faldskaus before the Germans came, and they didn't replace him with a German or a Quisling follower at first, so he was trying to get information about what was happening with the Allies. And so, he was put in the camp as a political prisoner, and he was lucky they didn't kill him for breaking their law about listening to enemy broadcasts. *Ja,* they killed people for trying to find out the truth. It was impossible to know what was happening, unless you knew people in the resistance who had networks.

Sigvard told a farmer who met him at the camp fence one day about the killings of political prisoners at Grini; and so, the farmer got word to us somehow. I don't know who came to talk to Papa, but he said Sigvard knew the men who tried to sabotage the hydro plant in Rjukan, and they were shot there, in the forest behind the camp.[40] So my father must have been too frightened to risk going to a camp. I think Papa was frightened of dying.

—Who wasn't frightened, mother? Do you think the Lidelskys weren't frightened? Do you think Samara wasn't?

—Papa thought he had no choice, Gudrun, he had a family to feed, to keep alive. The Germans were shooting people who didn't comply with orders, they were shooting random people in revenge for sabotage against them, they were burning whole villages in retaliation for attempted raids!

—Fear is an excuse.

—It's not an excuse, but an explanation. Fear is what makes people behave badly. I believe this now.

—What happened to Sigvard?

—After the war, Sigvard weighed about eighty pounds, and I didn't recognize him when he came to the house to recover. He was a bachelor, so my

---

40   The first attempt to sabotage the heavy-water plant failed, and the Norwegians involved were arrested and shot. The second effort, which was successful, was led by Joachim Rønneberg, who became, with his fellow resistance-fighters, a national hero. —SJ

mother nursed him. She sent me to the town hall to bring our radio back home. I saw the Lidelskys' radio there and I cried all the way home. I knew no one would be going there to get it.

—When did you know what happened to the Jews in Norway?

—I didn't know what happened until it was all over, a while after that even.[41]

—Let's back up, you haven't told me about the Lidelskys. Did they have to wear yellow stars?

—No, but they had to show their identification papers at the police station. All Jews in Norway did, citizens or not. The newspapers had notices ordering them to do this.

—*Why?*

—To have a black "J" stamped on them. To make it easier for the Germans to know who they were, if they were stopped somewhere and told to produce their papers.

—To give the police the right to mistreat them, you mean.

—That too.

—Did people know persecution was escalating in Norway?

—Of course. Businesses owned by Jews were being vandalized in the bigger cities. Nothing was being done in secret, regular Norwegians were

---

41 What the resistance knew, however, is under dispute as I write this; investigative journalists have suggested that the exiled government and the resistance knew what was coming months before the deportations of Norway's Jewish people on November 26, 1942, but did not warn them or try to save them (other than through individual acts of profiteering by those who took large sums from the wealthy, who gave all they had to buy their way to safety in Sweden). —SJ

involved by then. The seven hundred "J" rubber stamps were made for the Ministry of Police by a private Oslo rubber factory. They were paid for by the Ministry of Finance through the Norges Bank. And they were shipped to every police station across the country.

–So hundreds of people knew?

–More. Oh, many, many more than that.[42] Oof, my stomach, Gudrun, the pain!

–We'll stop now so you can rest.

[The daughter injects morphine into her mother's arm; the old woman winces, then shuts her eyes. They resume their conversation later when the drug has worn off enough for the mother to focus.]

–You were telling me about the Lidelskys, before. About the stamp in their papers.

–*Ja,* it was in the early days of the occupation. For the first two years the Lidelskys held their breath. They were Norwegian in every way, they'd been granted citizenship in 1925 after living there for twenty years, the country's rule for Jews in those days. Norway would protect them, they were certain of that![43] The Lidelskys, they ran away from Russia, and they had rebuilt their lives in Norway, twice. Oslo was frightening, Moritz said, with so

---

42 On December 1, 1942, the Norwegian exile government's foreign minister, Trygve Lie, advised the World Jewish Congress by letter that it was unnecessary for the Norwegian government to appeal to its people to fulfill their human duty towards the Jews in Norway. —SJ

43 Norway banned Jews from Norway in 1814 with a clause in its constitution, which was repealed in 1851. The Jewish community began to grow after this, when pogroms in Russia and the Baltics in the early twentieth century and Nazi persecution in the 1930s forced them to flee. —SJ

many Gestapo and businesses being shut down, but Faldskaus was such a small town.

—That safe feeling fooled them, then.

—*Ja*. And it fooled me, too. Sammi showed me the J in her papers. Her mother kept it in her purse with her own. Then she told me she and her mother and father had to do more paperwork, they had to fill in a special form at the police station in town.[44] All Jewish people in Norway had to fill out this form, like a special census. The special J stamp wasn't enough, the Germans were collecting personal information about everyone's occupations and property. But Moritz was still working—his factory kept our town working, what could happen to him? That's what I told Sammi—don't worry, this is just a formality, the Germans have their systems, but we won't let anything happen to you.

She said, "Maybe you're right, but Hermann's family has already gone to Sweden!" I knew when she said this that I had lost her already—she would be going to Sweden, too, to join Hermann. Oh, you wouldn't believe how selfish a lonely teenage girl can be. Because that's what I thought about—that she would be leaving Norway and me behind.

—Did she get away?

—She didn't get the chance. They closed the border to refugees, so no more trains were going across by the time her mother decided to get tickets.

---

44   The "Questionnaire for Jews in Norway" had to be filled out by all Jewish people beginning in February 1942, with copies kept by the local police, the Nasjonal Samling's Office of Statistics, and the Ministry of Police. The Office of Statistics' definition of a Jew: three out of four grandparents are fully Jewish. —SJ

Samara Lidelsky's Questionnaire for Jewish Norwegians [hyperlink]

Date: March 3, 1942

Questionnaire for Jewish Norwegians from Rogaland political district

Family name: Lidelsky
for women, also provide maiden name:
First name: Samara
Born (month, date, year): 10, 11, 1925
Country: Norge
Address: 19 Grønnevet Gate, Faldskaus, Norway
Religion: Jewish
Martial status: Unmarried
Date of marriage:
Did you marry into a Jewish family?
Number of children:

(Name)   (Age)

Current occupation: Student
Theoretical or Practical training:
Military education:
Public education:
Current student at academic organization: Sollia School
Former student at academic organization:
Member of foreign organization:
Nationality: Norwegian   Citizenship: Norway
Been in Norway since: Birth
Lived where before Norway: Nowhere

And so, one Tuesday morning, Moritz was arrested in Faldskaus by our town *lensmann*,[45] Erikssen.[46] We watched Moritz get pushed into the police car in front of his house, with Rebekka and Samara screaming after it in the street as it drove away.[47] The same day, possession of the Lidelsky house was officially taken because of the law Quisling passed. But Rebekka and Sammi stayed in their house, it took time for the Germans to get to the small towns to change locks on the doors.

Moritz's father Meyer had died before the war, and Leo left Faldskaus not long after the invasion, to help the British forces fight Hitler because he couldn't stand to do nothing. So, he left.

—How did he escape, with the Germans everywhere?

—He got to the coast, where a friend had a boat. Leo knew everyone, everyone liked Leo. It was dangerous to leave, but also it was illegal. The Lidelskys could have been arrested then for Leo's escape, if the Jews had been counted before he left.

And so, because Moritz was the only male Jew left in Faldskaus, he was arrested and sent alone by

---

45   *Lensmann* is Norwegian for sheriff.

46   On Monday, October 26, 1942, orders were issued that starting on October 27, 1942, all Jewish men over the age of fifteen were to be arrested and moved to Berg and Falstad concentration camps, and all property was to be confiscated, safety deposit boxes emptied, and bank accounts frozen. —SJ

47   As with all businesses owned by Jewish people, Moritz's business was taken over and eventually his factory, inventory, and fixtures were sold by the Quisling government—with subsequent funds going into an account in the Central Bank of Norway known as "the Joint Jewish Assets." According to the Norwegian Act of October 26, 1942, which was about the confiscation of property belonging to Jews, it was an entirely legal action. —SJ

train to Oslo. That was where most of the Jews lived and where all the other Jewish men in Norway were taken. And then they were all sent by bus and taxi to concentration camps.

—The Nazis used regular taxis?

—Driven by Norwegians, *ja*. Norwegian police and taxi drivers participated in the round up. Oh *ja*, Gudrun, I told you, there were Nazis in Norway before the Occupation! There were thousands of collaborators during the war, too. Some Norwegians even joined the German army and fought for Hitler. There were bad people in Norway too, then. The same everywhere in the world. Don't tell me you are in your fifties and you didn't know that, Gudrun.

—Well, I've never heard about Norwegian collaboration, only the resistance—

—There was resistance, there was opposition, but there was also the opposite.

—The opposite of opposition?

—This is what I'm telling you. You haven't heard the worst of it, Gudrun.[48]

[The daughter stands up and stretches, leaning her head back and closing her eyes. She pours water

---

48 Roughly 15,000 Norwegians volunteered for the German army; and roughly 16,000 other citizens collaborated with the Nazi occupation of Norway. Of the 2,173 Jewish people living in Norway in 1942 (approximately 1,800 of whom were citizens), 23 were executed or killed themselves; 50–70 who were married to "Aryans" were imprisoned in Berg concentration camp until the end of the war; 767 were deported (mostly to Auschwitz); 741 of these people were murdered, and only 26 survived. The remainder escaped to Sweden, several hundred assisted by the Norwegian underground via the "Carl Frederiksen Transport" (code name for organized smuggling of Jews to safety in Sweden). About ten individuals remained in hiding in the country. Two hundred and thirty entire Norwegian Jewish families were wiped out. —SJ

from a jug into the glass on the table and drinks some, then refills the glass and gives it to her mother to sip from.]

—When we started you said you were going to tell me about my father.

—I keep telling you, you need to hear everything first. Sit down, I can't think with you standing there.

[Daughter sits down.]

And so, Rebekka wouldn't let Samara go to school for many days after the arrest of Moritz. Also, she took Sammi with her when she walked to the police station to report each afternoon. Then she decided it was better for Sammi to be in school than at home hiding behind the curtains like a criminal. Samara said her mother sent her back because she didn't want her daughter to see her struggling to prepare meals for the two of them—the cook and the housekeeper had both left, since Moritz wasn't there to pay them anymore. Leo had said the British would be invading soon and getting rid of the Germans, so Rebekka held onto the hope that her son had planted in her before he left.

No one thought Norway would be involved in the war. We were supposed to be neutral, like Sweden—that was our king's position, our government's. But the Germans didn't believe the British would respect that, they thought the British would conscript the Norwegian soldiers. The Germans didn't believe the British would be so stupid, leaving us vulnerable like that! So they got to us first.

There were so many German soldiers in Norway, hundreds of thousands of them in such a small country. In Stavanger, many Germans were billeted in people's houses, some on boats in the harbour. They liked us Norwegians, not just for our looks, but I don't know why.[49]

—Probably because so many were complicit. Or passive, at least, like your father.

—You were not there. You don't know what you would do, if you were in my parents' shoes.

—Oh, I think I do, Mamma.

—You shouldn't judge them, Gudrun. I had to stop judging them after I got pregnant with you. Which I will get to soon, if you will stop interrupting me.

—Okay. So, what happened after Moritz was taken away?

—Well, the next month, orders were sent to go find all the other Jews, the younger teenage boys, the women and girls and children. To arrest all of them, like they did Moritz.

It was a Tuesday, November 26, when Erikssen came to the school looking for Samara. Papa opened the door to the classroom and let him in. But Samara didn't come to school that day.

—Lucky for her, since your father would have let her be arrested!

—He said he only let Erikssen in because Samara wasn't there.

—You believed him?

---

49   During World War II in Denmark, 77 out of 5,600 Danish Jews were executed in the camps, and only 11 of Finland's 2,300 Jews were killed in concentration camps. More Jewish people were helped, and helped earlier, in those countries than in Norway, so more people were able to escape to safety. In comparison over 30 per cent of the Norwegian Jews estimated to have been residing in Norway were exterminated. —SJ

—I wanted to. I did for a while. But I think he would have opened the door anyway.

—Why?

—The night before, it was a Monday night, I was in my room at home when I heard the knock at our door. It was Sammi's mother, Rebekka, asking my parents to take her and Samara to our camp in the mountains. Friends of theirs, some Gentiles in Stavanger, sent word to her by phone that Jewish women and children all over Norway were going to be arrested and sent away to concentration camps.

By then, people knew—*I* didn't know, but people did, adults knew that the Jews would die, they would be killed.[50] All I knew was Sammi would be gone, she would not be treated well, and I might never see her again.

And so, I ran downstairs and saw Mrs. Lidelsky. Oh, she was so beautiful, Rebekka. In the winter she wore fur coats and hats, and she looked very fancy compared to my mother standing in her cotton apron beside my father in his thick, hand-knit sweater. I became hysterical, pleading with my parents. In front of Samara's mother, I cried and pleaded something terrible. But my father ignored me. He said, "I am so sorry Mrs. Lidelsky, we cannot help," and she looked him in the eye, but he looked away. And she

---

50 On November 26, 1942, all Jewish women and children in Norway were arrested; that night the D/S Donau left Oslo with 530 Norwegian Jews on board. In Stettin, they were loaded onto railroad cars and after two and a half days the train arrived—via Berlin—at Auschwitz. The elderly, women, and children were sent directly to the gas chambers. Only nine survived. —SJ

looked at me and I went to her and hugged her as hard as I could, and then she left.

After the door was closed, I told my father I hated him. So he grabbed my arm and shouted, "How would they get there—by me? I cannot be absent from the classroom in the morning, Sigrid! I would be a suspect!"

"I could tell the others you are sick!" I said.

"And what will Mamma say when the police come to the house and I am not here in my sick bed? They would arrest her for lying and then they would come for me! They would shoot you and me and Mamma and your brothers for disobedience! We must save our own family first, Sigrid."

"What for?" I yelled back at him. "What *for*?"

[The two women sit in silence for a few minutes. The old woman is crying quietly and her daughter hands her fresh tissues. They stop for the day. Lights out.]

ACT III

—You told me the other day that Samara had a brother, that he left Faldskaus.
—Leo. Such a handsome boy. He played football with the other boys, but he also was a violinist, he played classical music. He kept books for his father's factory, he was smart, smart. He loved to dance. And he played big-band jazz music on the radio until it was taken from the home. I'd never heard such music before. My family was so stiff, so serious....

But Leo. Leo disappeared in October 1940. He said he was going to Oslo on business, but we found out later from the Brandviks that he escaped with their son, Gunnar. The two boys had been friends in school. Together, they went to an island north of Stavanger and they went across the North Sea in an old fishing boat. They landed in the Orkney Islands first and the Norwegian Consulate arranged for them to go to London. Gunnar called home once they got there. He said they joined the Royal Norwegian Air Force and were being shipped to Halifax, and then going by train to Toronto for training. There were so many of them that the training centre in the harbour there was known as "Little Norway."

And so, you won't believe this, but our landlady Mrs. Pulkki told me she met Leo. He and some other young men came to Sudbury to visit a friend when they were on weekend leaves during their training. This friend rented an apartment from our own Mrs. P. She remembered this when you and I moved to Sudbury, and she was asking about my life in Norway during the war. Leo was probably the only Jewish Norwegian training to be a pilot in Little Norway, she remembered that about him. I told her about my friend Samara in Faldskaus, and she remembered Leo talking about his sister Samara—it was such an unusual name, she knew I must be talking about Leo's sister. Such a small, small world….

Mrs. Pulkki knew all about Leo, and yet his parents knew nothing—not even his girlfriend heard from him, the love of his life. The Germans censored mail, so Leo couldn't write home.

–Mamma, did Leo find out what happened to his mother and sister? That they were sent to the camps?
–They weren't sent to the camps.
–No? What happened to them?
–Don't rush me, Gudrun. Please.
–Sorry. Go on.
–Ah, Leo… Mrs. Pulkki found out later from her tenant that Leo was shot down over Germany, when he took a risky bombing assignment in 1944. It was as if he wanted to go on a suicide mission, I think. The Germans got him too, in a way. But at least he went fighting.
–So the Germans did get Rebekka and Sammi, then?
–In a way they did, but I'm not ready to tell you about that yet.

I was so lonely in Faldskaus. I missed Sammi and her family so much. Their house, one of the nicest in Faldskaus, now belonged to the Germans. They would hold meetings there, sometimes, when regional leaders came. Before they used it though, when it was sitting empty, I would go there by myself sometimes. I knew where Samara kept a spare key behind the shrub at the back door. I would walk through the rooms and breathe in the air that still smelled like Rebekka's perfume. It was in the forgotten velvet curtains, which the Germans left hanging after clearing the house of most everything else.
Anyway, one day, he followed me.
–Who?
–His name was Heinrich. He was German.
–A German soldier?
–He fought for them, because Germany was his country. He had to join up.

–So they all said.

–I know you will judge me, Gudrun, but I was a young girl, I'd lost my best friend and—and—

–Go on, Mamma. This soldier was following you. And then what?

–The day he walked into Sammi's house and startled me, he said he was out for a walk and saw me go inside. I told him to leave and he said, "Is this your home?" He had learned basic Norwegian by then, it had been two years since the Germans came. "*Nei*," I told him, "*min venn*—" but I stopped, in case telling him about Sammi would make more problems for her, somehow.

He was such a gentleman. And so handsome. He said I was the most beautiful girl he had ever seen. I didn't wear make-up or red lipstick, like those girls who flirted with the soldiers. I was flattered. So we met at the Lidelskys' house, and—

–Mamma—hold on a minute. You were involved with a German soldier? How could you? After what happened to the Lidelskys, too! Your family must have hated you!

–Oh Gudrun, I know how bad it looked to everyone. My family would rather I'd have married a Swede or a Dane than be with Heinrich. My brothers wanted to beat him up when I started showing, but they knew they'd be arrested, so they hit me instead.

–Wait a minute—when you started showing? With me?

–Helmer slapped my face so hard that I dropped on the floor and then he and Per both kicked at my legs, screaming *tyskertøs! tyskertøs!* until Father told them to stop.

—Stop crying, Mamma, please, just talk to me. What does tyskertøs mean?

—Tyskertøs, the word is so ugly, it even sounds like a punishment, tsk tsk. "German girl," that's what it means, but really, a bad girl, a German's whore, more or less. Father was crying, watching the attack. But he didn't tell them to stop until they had really mopped the floor with me.

Every day after that, Helmer spat in my face. Per stopped speaking to me. To him I was dead, he didn't even see me in the house anymore, for the first time he left me alone.

[The daughter reaches toward her mother, who is sobbing, but her arm stops mid-air, and she repeats this gesture a few times before she is able to caress the old woman's arm, saying Shh, shh, shh, until she has cried herself to sleep.

The daughter sits in her living room, not knowing what to do with her rage—at her mother, but also at herself.... She has a negative visceral reaction to her own physical body: she wants to vomit herself up, purge her tissue of her genes, of the cells that carry her father's DNA. Her head pounds; she swallows four Tylenols, then spits them up, and continues to wretch even though her stomach is empty. She is screaming in her mind; she pictures herself standing in an empty field, leaning forward with her hands on her thighs, screaming into the air as loudly as possible until her voice hoarsens to silence. She realizes she is hyperventilating; her fingers, toes, then her arms and legs begin tingling, then go numb, and she faints.

She awakes a few minutes later, hearing her mother call out to her, like a child.]

–Gudrun! Gudrun!
–I'm here, Mamma.
–Gudrun, I'm sorry, I'm sorry, please Gudrun, please come here, I'm still me, it's me, Gudrun, it's me… .
[The daughter turns the tape recorder back on and speaks quietly into it while the old woman sleeps.]
–My name is Gudrun Johansen. I am going to talk with my mother in a few minutes, after I try to get her to eat a bowl of oatmeal. She is eating less and less, and she spits up what she does eat. Her heart is fluttering. Her body is shutting down.

I am finding this very difficult. My mother has kept herself so private, so apart from me, all her life, yet here I am, her nurse, her confessor—her conscience, it seems. Mamma seems to want to talk and talk and talk. I have never heard my mother talk so much as she has these last few days.

She is finally telling me stories about her life in Norway before I was born. About her family, her best friend, her brothers, and her lover. And so, it tuns out that my father was not a high-school-boyfriend-turned-fiancé, killed in the early days after Germany invaded. I am angry—angry that my mother lied to me my entire life, and angry that she felt she had to lie to me.

How am I going to tell Sam about this? I don't think I can.…
[Lights out.]

[When lights come back up, daughter is spoon-feeding her mother breakfast.]
–No more porridge, Gudrun, I can't swallow it. Maybe later I will try again.
–Okay Mamma. Let's try to pick up where we left off

last night. Do you remember what we were talking about?

—Some of it I remember telling you.

—You told me about your brothers' reactions to your getting pregnant. Tell me about your parents' reaction. Were you kicked out of the house?

—*Nei*, they didn't want me out of their sight. You can't imagine the gossip in a small town like Faldskaus. There was no privacy anywhere. My mother would not let me go out of the house.

—No wonder!

—I want you to know that I didn't flirt with Heinrich when I saw him following me. I wasn't that kind of a girl. In the cities, Heinrich told me, girls wore red lipstick and got dressed in their best and went for walks in the evenings, to meet them, the handsome soldiers. The soldiers were arrogant, they gave photographs of themselves to girls they met. It was a strange way of courting. The men had pistols on their hips, and many wore wedding rings, and there they were, parading about and flirting with girls. I suppose some girls were attracted to the power, the authority they carried with them.

—But they were the enemy. Your Heinrich was the enemy.

—*Ja,* but technically, they weren't fighting us Norwegians, once they settled into the country; they were there to keep order, like police officers, in a way.

—You sound like you are making excuses for yourself. Did you not know what was happening in the camps?

—My family did not talk about the news, the

Occupation. My brothers said they knew from their friends what was happening, in Germany and Poland, say, but my parents did not want to hear it.[51] Our dinner table was silent every night. There was a German soldier for every family in Norway, almost. We were not allowed to talk about what was happening, in case we were overhead criticizing the Germans. They said there were spies even in little Faldskaus....

–Never mind—I don't want to argue about that. I want you to tell me why you kept me, when you knew you were pregnant.

–Abortions weren't allowed by the Germans! They wanted pure-blooded Norwegian babies to become Germans, to resupply the Reich with the right kind of people! But I wasn't going to give you to Hitler, no matter what. There was a maternity home Heinrich told me about, where girls made pregnant by Germans were treated like royalty and

---

51 "What knowledge was available in the fall of 1942 about the fate awaiting the Norwegian Jews? What did the Norwegian exile authorities know? Finn Koren from the Norwegian embassy in Bern reported to Minister of Foreign Affairs Trygve Lie on 17 August 1942 that, 'The most gruesome reports are arriving from Poland about the treatment that the unfortunate Jews are being subjected to, and as far as what can be understood, they are trying to 'liquidate' the entire race. What is going on in Warsaw's ghettos defies description. About one third of the Jewish population over there is estimated to be dead.' With respect to the Jews from the Netherlands, Koren reported: 'A larger per cent is known with certainty to have been killed already—either by gas, which is probably the most efficient and quickest way, or by strychnine. Apparently Hitler believes that the Jews must be erased from the face of the earth, or at least from Europe, by any means necessary.' Dark chapter in the history of statistics?" by Espen Søbye, published at Statistics Norway website, October 2006. https://www.ssb.no/en/befolkning/artikler-og-publikasjoner/a-dark-chapter-in-the-history-of-statistics-1.

given all kinds of food we couldn't buy.[52] I didn't want to go there, I wasn't one of them. Those girls agreed to have Aryan babies for the Führer. Those women voluntarily went through screening processes to prove they had at least three generations of pure blood. Their babies became *property*, German property. Instead of names they had a Lebensborn number.

–They gave the babies a number, like they gave Jewish people numbers?

–*Ja*! They counted everything, the Germans. Babies were counted because they were going to be an asset to them, you see—

–So, to them, I was a thing, not a human being—

–Not you, you were not in the system. Besides, Heinrich was going to stay and marry me after the war, you see—

–You believed him? Your Nazi boyfriend?

---

52   Thirty thousand or more young Norwegian women—10 per cent of the population—dated Germans during the Occupation; thousands of women were arrested and interned after the war for collaboration. Eight thousand officially registered babies (and up to four thousand others) were born to them over the course of the war. Of these, one thousand, two hundred were born in *Lebensborn* homes (set up in requisitioned hotels and villas or as new builds) established and administered by the Nazis (*Lebensborn* meaning "fount of life"). In almost half of these cases, the paternity was undetermined, and most of the children were abandoned, to be raised in orphanages and mental institutions; two hundred were taken from the mothers and sent to Germany for adoption; one hundred were adopted by Norwegian parents, many of whom ill-treated them. (The Norwegian government tried to deport all the children to Germany but were prevented from doing so by the Allies). In institutions, the children were treated as if mentally deficient, suffered mental and physical abuse, and were not given schooling or other opportunities owed to citizens. A Norwegian in the Ministry of Social Affairs compared the children to rats in the cellar. —SJ

–Listen to me, Gudrun. This is not easy to tell you.
–And I wish you hadn't!
–You said you wanted to know about your father, you wanted to know everything!
–But I thought that he was Norwegian, your high-school sweetheart! That you were sent away because of the shame of not being married before you had me, that's all! That all sounds so innocent now! And ridiculous! I feel ridiculous, for thinking what I did about you all my life, about you and my imaginary father—
–Don't yell at me. Please. Please. I had to make a choice, Gudrun! Heinrich left me, left Norway. So to make a new life in Canada, to raise you alone, it was better I was known as a widow here. It was better to think that your father had died, than to have anyone know they called you terrible names back home.
–You should have told me!
–When was a good time to tell you? I had to forget so much, to keep going! On my own, alone in a new country, learning a new language, new people—everything! And with a young child! And you think you would have listened to me then, anyways? When you were young? Let me finish, Gudrun, please. Please, I need to get this out.
–But you let me brag about my father the hero, about our relatives being in the resistance, about you helping your Jewish best friend. You didn't save her!
–No. But I saved you. You could have been taken from me, deported to Germany even, to be adopted by a German family! If not that, you would have been bullied and labelled mentally deranged by our own government, because of who your father was! And I saved

myself. Yes, I did. And I was lucky to get out. In Norway I was considered garbage, worse than garbage.[53]

—How did you keep your secret, then?

—By hiding! For two years! We were never seen in a window, you *or* me—my parents made sure of that. Many girls were paraded through the streets after having their heads shaved. They were humiliated in public. They were treated worse than the Nazis by Norwegians. I was spared that, at least.

—I don't know who I am anymore. You told me made-up stories! Lies!

—And it helped, didn't it? You were proud of your father, the hero who died fighting on the right side! And it helped me to forget myself, because our stories became the truth.

—What did Mrs. Pulkki know about your life in Norway?

—Not even she knew the truth, Gudrun. Do you think she would have been so good to us if she'd known?

—So, you told her my father was a Norwegian resistance fighter, killed during a raid…

—Even I started to believe it, after a while. But you don't want to hear any more of this.

---

53 Near the end of the war the Norwegian government, exiled in London, broadcast warnings to collaborators in Norway, including messages intended for the women who'd been intimate with German soldiers: "We have previously issued a warning and we repeat it here of the price these women will pay for the rest of their lives: they will be held in contempt by all Norwegians for their lack of restraint." [Quote cited by Rob Sharp, "The chosen ones: the war children born to Nazi fathers in a sinister eugenics scheme speak out." Accessed at www.independent.co.uk/news/world/europe/the-chose...fathers-in-a-sinister-eugenics-scheme-speak-out-771017.html —SJ

—Mamma, I'm calmer now, not like last night. Maybe you can answer some of my questions.
—You look like you have no room in your heart for me, Gudrun.
—I feel like I don't even know you, Mamma!
—What else can I tell you?
—Let's go back to Sammi's story. What happened after your father said no to Rebekka?
—Oof, Sammi. Okay. The next morning. I told you already about Erikssen coming to the school in his little red car; he probably wanted to get Sammi in first, so Rebekka would be easier to pick up. And so, after he left our classroom without Sammi, he went to the Lidelsky house: no one home. Next, he went over to our house—everyone knew how close Sammi and I were, it was natural to think my mother might know something. She was afraid of being accused of helping them escape, so she told him about Rebekka's visit to us the night before. Imagine, telling the authorities that you didn't help save someone's life, because it would score a point for you—but that's how it was, that is what she did. So Erikssen had one more idea. He went to the factory.
—Moritz's business? Wasn't it shut down?
—No, it was taken over, it was modified to make furniture for barracks and other things the Germans needed. The men still worked there every day, they still took home their wages, as if nothing had changed. They liked Moritz, they were not happy when he was arrested, but they also had families to feed.
And so, Erikssen went there that morning, to see if the men knew anything about Rebekka and Sammi,

but when he got there, he saw the workers building two coffins. And they were weeping. *Weeping*, they were grown men, weeping as they worked.
–Why? I don't understand—
–Because Rebekka and Sammi, they'd gone to the factory in the middle of the night, and… and… and they—
–They what?
–They hanged themselves. From the rafters.

JUNE

While I work through my mother's archives, I gradually learn to control the loathing and confusion that initially fogged my mind by thinking of it as a kind of fuel, as a form of energy that might convert the awful truth into something good, by turning silence and ignorance into something useful, like knowledge.

I am angry, very angry at my mother, for not letting me in on the story until now. She should not have kept secret what she learned from Besta for as long as she did; had she shared the information she'd gleaned before my grandmother's death, which was over five years ago now, I might have taken a different direction in my life than I did. I might, years ago, have become the person I am beginning to be, rather than continuing to work blindly in a café, ignoring history, my own and my family's history. Because now that I have the information that Besta provided, I have to *do* something with it.

So yes, I am angry. Or was. But the stories themselves are convincing me to accept my mother's reticence, her secrecy, and to understand a little of how she must have felt when she found out the truth. And I am grateful to her for giving me the opportunity—not only to learn who I came from, but also to explore what that information means, to me and to my future.

So I keep my promise to my mother, and I forgive her everything.

In the spring I applied to interdisciplinary graduate programs in history writing, citing my interest in European family narratives that are only now emerging from the third generation post-World War II. It's my generation, which did not live through the war—which did not even grow up hearing stories *about* the war—we are the ones who need to do the research; to dig up details about how family members who *were* there, and their peers and politicians of the day, behaved; and to tell it....

When I finish the project, maybe I should think about confessing it all to J. I was so judgmental about his German family's history, questioning Otto and Grete's wartime pasts. I praised my own grandmother for being good and kind, while telling J. that his grandparents might have been Nazis. I criticized J. and his father for not looking into Otto's experience as a soldier, and then into the provenance of the artwork Grete's wealthy family acquired in Berlin; yet I held out my own family, my Norwegian relatives, as heroes, almost—as people who would do whatever was necessary to help other human beings.

The shame I feel imagining this conversation with J. makes me understand my mother's reluctance to tell me about our own family background for so long.

I call Fern, instead, and confess to my Jewish friend that I carry the genes of a Nazi German officer. I ask her to read my blog before we talk again.

"Oh. My. God."

"I know."

"Sam, this is unbelievable! Your grandfather was in Hitler's army, and your own mother didn't know? And your grandmother's family, they turned away their Jewish neighbours? This is like a movie. Your grandmother could have been writing a script for Hollywood, for god's sake! I've never heard anything about Norway and the Holocaust. I mean—I don't even know what to say to you right now."

But Fern is encouraging, too—she thinks I should do more research, whether I get into the graduate program or not.

JULY

A few weeks after I post "Generational Conversations," I begin to make contact on Facebook with relatives in Norway. I think of it as putting feelers out over the internet to test the vibes between families on either side of the ocean; I imagine, each time that I do this, that I am plucking the thick, sixth string of a guitar, tightening its tension and adjusting the low-pitched sound, hoping it will eventually be in key.

I have yet to tell my mother that I am investigating the family tree in this way.

And I haven't told these Norwegian relatives about "Generational Conversations," either. I don't want to preempt their receptivity by having them shut me out before I have a chance to speak with them.

Tonight, I log into Facebook and send a direct message to the third cousin who runs his father's hotels. My cousins live in the suburb of a small city on the south coast—not far, I don't think, from the Lukas tribe's original homestead. They own most of the hotels in the area now. Karl has been the friendliest of the cousins on Facebook, and he has invited me to come and stay with his family sometime.

Me: Hey, Karl. How are things?

Karl is also on Facebook now—the green dot next to his name and photo tells me this, so I stay online and wait for his reply. Underneath my message, I see little circles bobbing up and down like drunk ellipses, which mean Karl is typing out an answer to me.

Karl: Busy. Our newest property is taking most of my time, and there are so many problems with our foreigners, you wouldn't believe what we're going through.

Foreigners? Maybe the equivalent word in Norwegian isn't an anachronism, I think; maybe it just sounds funny when it's translated to English?

Me: Aren't most of your guests from other places?

Karl: I don't mean tourists, I mean the refugees we take in. The government pays us to let them live here and eat in the restaurant.

I'd read that Norway has recently taken in many refugees from the Middle East and Africa. There was an article in the paper recently about a young boy from the Congo—who'd had his arm cut off by rebels for refusing to shoot any more people in a village they were raiding—who had moved to Kirkenes, in the far north, where it is either day or night, one or the other, for much of the year. But I didn't know hotels were being used as temporary housing.

Me: Wow, that must be very difficult for them.

Karl: I don't think living in a hotel for free is difficult!

Me: I mean being outsiders, having no choice about anything.

Karl: No. It's us with no choice. We have to take them in.

I imagine the shadow families living in Karl's hotels, slinking into the dining room as waiters and waitresses fawn and fuss over the other, tipping customers. I think of the boy from the Congo, arriving in a town that is white and cold no matter what time of year. I imagine myself arriving in his home village, with only one arm and not speaking the local language, being stared at and dismissed as lazy by the community, while waiting for the system to place me in a language program.

I don't think I want to stay with Karl when I go to Norway someday.

WHAT'S IN A NAME?
AN INTERVIEW WITH MY MOTHER

Posted July 22, 2007, on
samarajohansen.ca

Samara Johansen: Tell me why you named me Samara.

Gudrun Johansen: It was to make my mother happy. I'd heard very little about her friend Samara when I was growing up, but I knew she had been someone my mother had loved. I knew Mamma had not had a good relationship with her parents, and that she never found a friend in Canada like her childhood friend Sammi. I also knew she longed for Norway my whole life, that she'd be homesick forever. So I thought the gesture would be comforting to Mamma.

SJ: Maybe it was. Maybe it brought back happy memories.

GJ: That's what I'd hoped. But now that I know everything, I don't think so. Can you imagine the pain she must have felt, hearing your name? Every time she said your name, or heard me say it, she must have felt terrible.

SJ: You couldn't have known. She didn't tell you anything!

GJ: I know, but still.

SJ: Anyway, how did you manage having me and working as a single mother?

GJ: When you were born, Mamma was still living in Sudbury. I'd moved to Copper Cliff a few years before—I made good money at Inco, compared to the jobs I could find in Sudbury. I didn't want Mamma to move in to help out, so I saved what I could from my salary so I could take time off work to be home with you as a newborn. There were no paid maternity leaves in those days—back in the nineteen-seventies, ages ago! My employers at Inco were kind, considering they could have replaced me permanently. Instead, I was allowed to stay home for three months, which was all I could afford, and then I had to find someone to babysit for me while I was at work, until you started kindergarten.

SJ: Oh, I remember, that smelly, large woman who watched soap operas all afternoon and forced us to dress up in costumes she'd made herself and act out weddings.

GJ: What? You never told me that!

SJ: I didn't?

GJ: No! You made a fuss when I dropped you off at her house, I remember that—I had to bribe you with trips to the candy store to make you stop screaming and go through her door. But no wedding story. I would have remembered that. And told her to stop, too.

SJ: Maybe I knew that, and I didn't want you to make it worse.

GJ: I wouldn't have had much choice but to leave you there anyway. There weren't professional daycares, like there are now.

SJ: And you had to work.

GJ: Yes and no. I could have gone on social assistance. But I worked because I wanted to. I'd only known women who worked. My mother's life was difficult, but she did what she had to do, to raise me. She didn't owe anyone anything, she didn't have to feed a husband or get his permission to buy things, for instance. Not that she had extra cash very often.

SJ: So now I know why Besta had you. Why did you have me?

GJ: You were conceived out of negligence, pure and simple. The man I was dating didn't have a condom and we were both reckless types, and, well, that's how you came to be.

SJ: And he didn't want to get married?

GJ: No, but I didn't either!

SJ: I know about your job at the university. But what was your job at Inco like?

GJ: I can't tell you that, Sam—I was sworn to secrecy, no matter who was asking.

SJ: It was medical records, not CSIS!

GJ: Yes, but information used to be kept from people as if it were a matter of national security back then. No one was given their own records, and you could only get information about test results from the doctor. It was worse in Copper Cliff, being a company town. The doctor, Dr. Bain, he was a company employee.

SJ: So the company knew more about your health than you did.

GJ: There were benefits, too, to that relationship. Dr. Bain attended to me right away when my water broke, just before quitting time. I was moved from the office to the hospital as easily as if I'd planned it that way. And he delivered you.

SJ: That gives him way more credit than he deserves, to say he "delivered" me. You did that.

[Gudrun laughs.]

SJ: What was Besta's reaction when you got pregnant with me?

GJ: Remember what she said on the tape, about us both being single mothers?

SJ: Yes, I do. "A new family tradition," she called it.

GJ: Exactly. Well, that was at the end of her life, and she was looking for forgiveness from me, by then. But she wasn't so *blasé* about it at the time, believe me. I'd humiliated her, she said. We were immigrants, we had to be better than Canadians or we'd never be accepted, *et cetera et cetera*. This, after we'd lived here for almost thirty years!

SJ: Who was Mrs. Pulkki?

GJ: She was our landlady. She owned the apartment building Mamma and I lived in. She lived in a three-bedroom suite on the top floor, facing the street, and we lived in a one-bedroom on the first, facing the parking lot, just like I am now. But on the first floor, we had headlights that pierced our curtains at night and early in the morning.

Anyway, Mrs. Pulkki didn't have any children, and she took a liking to me. She babysat when Mamma was out working, until I was old enough to start school. She took me with her to stores and introduced me to everyone we met as Gudrun Pulkki. She wasn't always kind to other people, but she was the best friend my mother had in Canada.

SJ: Did you ever see a picture of your father?

GJ: Once. Unfortunately. In the one photograph Mamma had—she finally showed it to me, before she died—he has medium-brown hair, straight and dull, and puffy bags under his eyes. That's where I get them from. My mother was beautiful, and you are beautiful; but me, I look like my father. I have his wide philtrum, too—you know, the space under your nose? And it's getting worse with age, as if gravity is pulling it down. I keep biting my top lip all the time now, it just keeps getting in the way! I wish I'd never seen that picture. It would be easier to have no image of him in my mind.

SJ: You didn't put the picture in the box you gave me at Christmas.

GJ: I tore it up, after Mamma told me the whole story. But you can't unsee what you've already looked at.

SJ: Did you try to contact your father, after Besta told you the truth about him?

GJ: What do you think, Samara?

SJ: You only call me Samara when you're angry.

GJ: You know better than to ask me that. I assumed he was dead, anyway. He was older than Mamma.

SJ: Have you thought of looking up any of your cousins in Norway?

GJ: Absolutely not! I have no idea who they are, what kind of people they might be. Or what they would think of me. I doubt they know about my existence, even, from what my mother told me about her brothers. They married girls from Oslo, not locals, so their wives wouldn't have heard any of it. Oh, I suppose my uncles might have said they'd had a sister who moved to Canada, maybe they'd have said that much—but nothing about me, or about Mamma having a baby by a German. I'm sure that would have been kept secret.

AUGUST

I've spent much of this summer reading about what happened to the *tyskertøser,* and to the *Lebensborn* children in Norway. I became grateful that Besta got away and brought my mother to northern Ontario to grow up. No paradise, to be sure, far from family and the familiar, but also far from the pain that would have been inflicted on them, had they stayed.

Then, online, I found a white paper commissioned by the Norwegian government that reviewed the recommendations of a committee on how to compensate Jewish survivors of liquidated estates—a committee that was created in 1996, over fifty years after the end of the war. I read that the government's Reparations Office continued economic persecution of the few Jewish survivors and their estates ("beneficiaries") after the war by taxing property and charging administrative fees, sometimes beyond the value of the estates themselves—so survivors or relatives of murdered Jewish families were punished instead of compensated. [54]

---

54   An inheritance tax, lower for direct heirs than for more distant relatives, was applied, and an order of inheritance was created "based on who had died first in a family that entered the gas chamber together." White paper no. 82 (1997-98): Historical and moral settlement of the Jewish minority during World War II, p. 7. —SJ

I realize now that, had there been any Lidelsky family members left—an uncle or cousin, say, somewhere in the family tree—then the house Besta played in with her friend, the house where she conceived my mother, in fact, would not have been inherited by that cousin or uncle, but would have been sold to cover the costs of administering its mortgage and taxes in the years since Moritz was arrested, deported, and killed.

It's horrific, simply horrific, the extent to which people will go to harm each other. I still have so much to learn.

On my way to work on Tuesday afternoon, I stop at the bank to take some money from the ATM. There are two machines there, but one is out of commission. As I punch my PIN into the keypad, a man enters the glass vestibule and stands what feels like two inches behind me.

I am instantly irked by his invasion of the bubble of privacy that people usually give each other when waiting in line. I half turn and look at the guy's broad, unshaved face, framed by sideburns that have not been in style for at least ten years. He is younger than me; he has dark, deep-set eyes and shaggy hair, which is mashed flat on the left side of his head as if he'd just gotten out of bed. He is over six feet tall and staring down at me, scowling. I ask him to move back a little, but he stays put.

"What's your problem?"

"You are, bitch."

I quickly glance through the window at the three tellers sitting behind the counter inside the bank, to see if anyone might be looking, but no luck. I think about my options: Bang on the glass to get help? Continue with my transaction, withdraw the money, and leave? Tell him I won't continue unless he backs off? None of those felt safe. I hit the cancel button and step aside; the man puts his card in, gets his cash, then leaves without looking back.

I am shaking as I reinsert my card and get my cash. I think about reporting the incident to the bank manager inside, but what would I say, that a rude man frightened me? And what would I expect the manager to do—look at a video of the scene that took place in the vestibule, identify and call the customer, and chastise him for being an asshole? And if the guy lives in my neighbourhood, then what? There would be retribution the next time he saw me, I'm sure of that.

No, I decide that I did the right thing. I didn't give in to him; I took myself out of harm's way.

So why does it continue to bother me?

"It's stupid, I know," I tell Fern over a beer that night at a pub near Yonge and Bloor, halfway between our homes, where we often meet. "You'd think the guy assaulted me."

"He did," Fern says. "He threatened you with his body language and his words. He violated your right to use the ATM without him breathing down your neck, insulting you and getting you out of the way so he could get his money out first. A woman-hating bully, that's what he was."

"I feel like I didn't stand up for myself."

"Your instinct kicked in: Save Thyself. Nothing wrong with that."

But I'm not so sure.

"You think you could have taught this jerk a lesson, or reformed him somehow, with words? It's not like you to blame the victim, Sam."

"It's not about blame, it's more nuanced than that. I'm trying to figure out how fear can make a person act, or not act. There was no one else there, which is why I felt so afraid, but if someone else was waiting in line, would they have said anything to help me out? Or if it were happening to someone in front of me, would I step in then? Because I honestly don't know. I *think* I would stand up for someone else more easily than I could for myself, but I might not do anything. Like all those people in Europe who didn't help their Jewish neighbours when they were being persecuted, because they were afraid they'd be punished."

"Did I ever tell you what my mother said when I was in high school and wanted to go to a party outside our neighbourhood? 'Before you make a Gentile friend, ask yourself if that person would hide you.' She did, seriously!" Fern pats my arm, then says, "I think you would hide me, Sam."

I hope she's right.

Making room in my closet for a three-shelf bookcase I picked up on the curb, I find the bag full of clothes I brought over from J.'s apartment a year and a half ago. J. has been living in Upton Bay for over a year now and I am sure he doesn't need or want the items; he will have refreshed his wardrobe on his father's dime, shopping at the men's store on Main Street ever since moving in with his father, John.

Nonetheless, today is my day off, so I put J.'s belongings in my old VW and drive to Upton Bay. The traffic is not as bad as it was last August, and I pull into John's driveway earlier than I'd expected to.

"What's this?" J. asks when he opens the door, as if I were holding actual bag of garbage on the front porch of the house.

"Your stuff, what else?" I say, handing it to him. "Can I come in? I won't stay long."

In the kitchen, at the breakfast bar, I gulp down a glass of ice water. I notice J. is wearing a Lacoste shirt, the alligator logo sitting pertly above his left breast, and unevenly dyed Hugo Boss jeans with a stylish tear at the knee.

"You look well," I say. J.'s face is slimmer than it had been—he came off the prednisone, he tells me, in the spring.

"You'll be happy to know I'm not smoking anymore, by the way."

"For your health?"

"No! I just got sick of the smell in the house, in my clothes," he says, pulling at his collar. "And my teeth are staying whiter. It's important when you're performing to look good, especially around here."

"J., I really came because I owe you an apology."

I tell him about "Generational Conversations," about discovering who I really am, genetically speaking, about who my grandfather was. I tell him about some of the research I've done about how the Norwegian government treated babies like my mother.

"I read about a doctor advising the Minister of Social Affairs after the war about the limited potential of the children who were born to Norwegian girls and women. He called them mentally deficient and compared them to 'rats in the cellar.'"

"Jesus."

"I know, right? There is so much irony there, it's sickening. So, you were right after all, about Norwegians being the same as everyone else," I say.

I tell J. that I am starting my part-time Interdisciplinary Studies MA in Scandinavian Historiography in September on a mature-student scholarship. The university awarded me a travel bursary for next spring to help me research postwar treatment of Norwegian mothers and the Lebensborn in Norway, and the language and philosophy behind policy decisions. He seems sincerely happy for me, and there is no lingering resentment between us; it's about as clean a break as you can hope for. We could remain friends, but probably won't, and that's okay.

As I drive away, I think how different I am now, compared to last summer when J. and I came to Upton Bay together. I knew so little, and thought I knew so much—about J., about myself, about people, about the world. So very little!

I am really looking forward to starting my program. It can include a creative component, so for this part of the degree I want to interview my relatives about what they know of their parents' and grandparents' experiences during World War II. My plan is to write a novella, building on "Generational Conversations" using their stories and my research to demonstrate a principle of historiography that I have started to think about and formulate:

> Like flowstone—a translucent curtain of minerals that forms when water trickles down cave walls, both preserving and creating a record—the past exists in the present through the accumulated voices that tell its stories, layer by layer, generation by generation. Only by uncovering these traces can the truth emerge, from the distance of time.

The distance of time: what a complex phrase that is, ascribing physical space to the concept of history. Time is a tool humans invented to measure change. The opposite of time is not timelessness but silence, change unaccounted for. To choose silence is to bury blame and shame. There has been enough of that in my family, I think, both in Canada and in Norway.

When I go to Norway, when I am there, I want to find the brass blocks called stumbling stones[55] —*snublesteiner*, in Norwegian—that have been placed in front of the Lidelsky home in Faldskaus.

> HER BODDE
>
> **SAMARA LIDELSKY**
>
> FØDSELSÅR 1925
>
> DØD 1942

> HER BODDE
>
> **REBEKKA LIDELSKY**
>
> FØDSELSÅR 1900
>
> DØD 1942

---

55   In the mid-1990s, German artist Gunter Demnig began to create memorial stumbling stones (*Stolpersteine* in German) for Holocaust victims and installing them in front of their last known address. Passersby "stumble" upon them, compelled to read the names and fates of real Jewish people who lived in the community until they were murdered or deported and killed in a concentration camp during World War II. The project has since spread to several European countries, including Norway. —SJ

> HER BODDE
>
> **LEO LIDELSKY**
>
> FØDSELSÅR 1919
>
> DØD 1944

> HER BODDE
>
> **MORITZ LIDELSKY**
>
> FØDSELSÅR 1899
>
> DEPORTERT 1942
>
> AUSCHWITZ
>
> DREPT JANUAR 1943

Back home after my visit to Upton, I am surprised to see my landlord Tim's cat, Lilly, outside the bay window of my apartment. Tim adopted her from a rescue group, and her tail is half gone; she has scars on her head and her haunches, and she trusts no one, not even the man who rescued her.

Clever Lilly has been known to open Tim's screen door—she can stand up on her hind legs and push a paw down on the handle, until the catch releases. Once free, she used to like to climb one of the posts on Tim's front deck to reach my balcony, then push through the broken window screen to be petted by J. For him, Lilly would purr demurely and do a first-rate, feline flirt act. But she hasn't been up to visit for a long, long time.

As I slide up the lower pane of glass to let Lilly in, a wall of hot humid air hits me in the face. Lilly steps through the torn screen as if I'd laid out a red carpet: head held high, dainty little steps over the sill and onto the table, down to the chair, then the floor. She mewls, searching the place inch by inch for J. I imagine her thinking: *His smell is here, but he isn't—how can that be?*

Lilly heads down the narrow hallway to the galley kitchen and stands in front of the refrigerator. "Are you hungry, Lill?" I ask, pushing Lilly gently aside with my foot so I can open the door and give her some coffee cream. Lilly immediately jumps up onto the lowest shelf, empty but for a carton of eggs, and collapses in a coil with her head resting on her front paws—as if cooling off in a fridge is the most natural thing in the world for a cat to do.

I wedge a heavy kitchen step stool in front of the door to prop it open. "You're such a strange girl, Lilly." I pat her head, and Lilly lets me.

I remember how bad the heat was last August, how my skin clung to the car seat when I took J. for drives. How sticky it was that week we stayed with Otto and Shelley in Upton Bay, and how airless the upstairs bedroom I stayed in was while J. slept soundly on the cooler first floor below. How the tourists at Evil Maple Estates waved their brochures in front of their faces as they disembarked from the air-conditioned buses and headed into the shop to taste varieties of wine and buy duty-free bottles, while the workers, like Matias, sweated for hours between the rows of grapevines, out of sight behind the sales centre.

I received an email last week from Matias, who attached a picture of his wife standing in front of their house, with chickens running free. He's kept in touch all year; I told him about my efforts last September, advocating for better laws and conditions for foreign agricultural workers. It was too late for Matias, though. He was sent home last fall when the infection in his hand worsened, and he wasn't approved to return in the spring. I thought about doing an article for the Upton *Town Crier* about the lack of fairness farmers show toward their temporary workers; but the editor I pitched it to told me he wouldn't publish it. It would be bad for the local economy, he said, to criticize a stalwart member of the community.

    J. had called me a "born-again bleeding heart" when I told him about Matias's wound and the conditions he was living under. He said I was coming late to the party ("and that's with a capital P," he added), and that it was ridiculous to think I could intervene or change the system. Now I wonder whether J. imagined Matias to be a good-looking competitor? J. did take Otto's side when I said the winery owner was uncompassionate and greedy. Maybe that was a bit much, I think now, considering the guy was a friend of Otto's and Otto was my host, but I was so angry! And I could have said a lot worse....

    I still remember Matias's badly injured hand, even the smell of it—the oozing cut that began at the fleshy base of his suntanned thumb and ran halfway across his palm. It has finally healed, he said, leaving a wide scar.

    I rub my index finger around my dry lips—with my fair colouring, I am forever moisturizing with sunblock and balms and gels, year-round—and the layer of new skin uncovered once the dead cells are gone smells faintly like steak, I think (or at least like my memory of the way raw meat smells). I know the human body replaces each of its cells every thirty days or so, and I wonder if that's what I'm noticing: the smell of that transition point, where death gives way to the living.

The cat jumps out of the fridge and screams her meows, as if accusing me of getting rid of J.

"Silly Lilly," I say, using J.'s nickname for her. "You're still heartbroken, aren't you?" Lilly lowers her head, tilting it, and makes a sound like a sigh; I swear the creature can understand English. Then she trots back to the window and pushes through the screen flap that has never been fixed, and she's gone.

I look out and see rush-hour traffic piled up right and left at the intersection, while vehicles going north and south crawl through it. Inside each car an entire world exists, the driver a nerve centre connected invisibly to family and friends and problems and joys. The driver in queue to turn left is honking at the car ahead, urging it to get through the intersection before the light changes, not wanting to be held up or kept from whatever it is he is driving toward—and then the light does change, and a large truck comes screeching to a halt just beyond my view. I hear a loud crash, then silence. For three long seconds, this corner of downtown is quiet, completely quiet, and then it all starts up again.

Life.

RESOURCES

While researching occupied Norway in World War II, I read several works (both fiction and nonfiction) that helped me to imagine what life might have been like for my characters. I'd like to acknowledge these texts here:

Aderet, Ofer. "New Book Leaves Norway's 'Heroic Role' in the Holocaust in Tatters." *Haaretz*, December 22, 2018. This article reviews Marte Michelet's 2014 Norwegian language book, the title of which translates as *The Greatest Crime: Victims and Perpetrators in the Norwegian Holocaust*.

Donner, Rebecca. *All the Frequent Troubles of Our Days: The True Story of the Woman at the Heart of the German Resistance to Hitler*. New York: Little, Brown and Company, 2021.

Eisen, Max. *By Chance Alone*. Toronto: HarperCollins Publishers, 2017.

Erpenbeck, Jenny. *Visitation*. Trans. Susan Bernofsky. New York: New Directions, 2010.

Fallada, Hans. *Every Man Dies Alone*. Trans. Michael Hoffman. Brooklyn: Melville House Publishing, 2009.

Hauge, Jens Chr. *The Liberation of Norway.* Trans. Marius Hauge. Oslo: Gyldendal Norsk Forlag, 1995.

Heivoll, Gaute. *Across the China Sea*. Trans. Nadia Christensen. Minneapolis: Graywolf Press, 2017.

Helmersen, Hanna Aasvik. *War and Innocence: A Young Girl's Life in Occupied Norway (1940-1945).* Seattle: Hara Publishing, 2000.

Ledermen, Marsha. *Kiss the Red Stairs: The Holocaust, Once Removed*. Toronto: McClelland & Stewart, 2022.

Maier, Ruth. *Ruth Maier's Diary: A Young Girl's Life Under Nazism*. Ed. Jan Erik Vold. Trans. Jamie Bulloch. London: Harvill Secker, 2009.

Ministry of Justice and the Police. "White Paper No. 82 (1997–98): Historical and moral settlement of the Jewish minority during World War II." From the government. no website, https://www.regjeringen.no/en/dokumenter/white.paper.no.82.1997-98/id21553/

Modiano, Patrick. *Dora Bruder*. Trans. Joanna Kilmartin. Oakland: University of California Press, 1999.

Olsen, Audun J. "Shippensburg University professor lived through the German Occupation of Norway." http://www.olsenhome.com/norway/

Petterson, Per. *Out Stealing Horses.* Trans. Anne Born. London: Vintage Books, 2006.

Sæland, Frode. "Herman Hirsch Becker: A microhistory, Parts I and II" (Scandinavian Jewish Forum, 2014 and 2017) (scandinavianjewish.blogspot.com). Published in Norwegian as *Herman Beckers Krig: Historien om familien Becker og jødene i Rogaland under andre verdenskrig.* Oslo: Aschehoug, 2009.

Seiffert, Rachel. *The Dark Room.* Toronto: Vintage Canada, 2002.

Sem-Sandberg, Steve. *The Tempest.* Trans. Anna Paterson. London: Faber & Faber Ltd, 2019.

Søbye, Espen. *Kathe—Always Been in Norway: The war destiny of an ordinary girl.* Trans. Kerri Pierce. Oslo: Krakiel Publishing, 2019.

Søbye, Espen. "Jewish Persecution During World War II: A Dark Chapter in the History of Statistics?" Trans. Lynn Nygaard. Statistics Norway, October 27, 2006.

Stenge, Margrit Rosenberg. "Narrow Escape to and from Norway." *Memoirs of Holocaust Survivors in Canada*, Vol. 29. Montreal: Concordia University Chair in Canadian Jewish Studies and the Montreal Institute for Genocide and Human Rights Studies, 2004.

Stratigakos, Despina. *Hitler's Northern Utopia: Building the New Order in Occupied Norway.* Princeton: Princeton University Press, 2020.

NOTES ON CHARACTER DEVELOPMENT

The character Moritz Lidelsky was inspired by my readings about the life, career, and death of Moritz Moses Rabinowitz. Born in 1887 in Poland, Rabinowitz was a retail merchant and philanthropist based in the city of Haugesund; there and in other towns and cities, including Stavanger and Kristiansand, he employed hundreds of people in his manufacturing company and built a hotel and a concert hall for his community. An outspoken critic of Nazism and anti-Semitism in Norway, his capture was a priority of the Gestapo, who arrested and jailed him in Stavanger in February 1941, and eventually deported him on the MS *Monte Rosa* on May 22, 1941. He was taken to Sachsenhausen concentration camp where he was killed on February 27, 1942.

The character of Leo Lidelsky is based on the life, military experience, and death of Herman Hirsch Becker, whose parents had immigrated from Russia in 1916 and settled in Stavanger. Herman was born in Norway, as were his brother and sister, and the family attained Norwegian citizenship after the required twenty years of residency. (Rebekka Lidelsky's character is loosely based on Herman's mother Judith, who played piano, gave lessons, and played in accompaniment to the silent movies screened at the local cinema.) Soon after the Occupation began, Herman fled Norway with a group of other young men (via a fishing vessel) to Scotland, then on to London, where Herman joined the Royal Norwegian Air Force. As a new recruit, he was sent to Halifax by boat, then to Toronto by train, to be trained as a pilot at the Royal Norwegian Air Force Training Centre, also called "Little Norway." He continued training in Scotland and Ireland and flew antisubmarine searches above Iceland and the Faro islands. He was flying with an Australian Commonwealth squadron in March 1945, bombing Gestapo headquarters in Denmark, when his plane went down, and Herman was drowned.

ACKNOWLEDGMENTS

My thanks to Aimée Parent Dunn for her editing expertise and vision, and to the talented Palimpsest Press team for making this book a reality.

For their ongoing support of my work, much gratitude to writer friends including Ian Colford, Kasia Jaronczyk, Dawn Promislow, Elise Levine, and Danila Botha.

I am indebted to Norwegian relatives who encouraged me to write about the Norwegian Holocaust and its aftermath in Norway, especially Berge-Andreas Steinsvåg and Sofie Margrethe Selvikvåg.

Much appreciation to Victoria Fox, Permissions Manager at Farrar, Straus and Giroux/Macmillan in New York, New York, for her tremendous help in licensing my use of Derek Walcott's poem as an epigraph to this novel.

Steven Schwinger, Historian with the Canadian Museum of Immigration at Pier 21 in Halifax, provided historical information and insights into the post-war circumstances faced by Norwegian immigrants to Canada. For his expertise and assistance, I am very grateful.

TITLE

The title is a phrase from a Derek Walcott poem that appeared in *The New York Review of Books* under the heading "This Page Is A Cloud" (December 6, 2007). The poem is listed as "Untitled (no. 54)" in *White Egrets* (London: Faber and Faber, 2010). It is also untitled in *The Poetry of Derek Walcott 1948-2013* (London: Faber and Faber, 2014; New York: Farrar, Straus and Giroux, 2017).

EPIGRAPHS

#54 "This page is a cloud between whose fraying edges" from THE POETRY OF DEREK WALCOTT 1948-2013, selected by Glyn Maxwell. Copyright © 2014 by Derek Walcott. Reprinted by permission of Farrar, Straus and Giroux and by Faber and Faber Ltd. All Rights Reserved.

Anton Chekhov's "Gooseberries" (1898) is in the public domain. The excerpt cited is from Anton Tchekoff, *The House with the Mezzanine and Other Stories,* translated by S.S. Koteliansky and Gilbert Cannan, published by Charles Scribner and Sons (1917), available at https://www.gutenberg.org/files/27411/27411-h/27411-h.htm#GOOSEBERRIES

Image on page 165 is "Monkey in doodle simple style on white background" designed by brgfx on Freekpik, used courtesy of www.Freepik.com.

BOOK-CLUB QUESTIONS: *A TOWN WITH NO NOISE* BY KAREN SMYTHE

1. Review the epigraphs at the front of the book. What is the connection between the Walcott poem, which provides the title of the novel, and the narrative voice?

2. What does the epigraph excerpt from the Chekhov story "Gooseberries" tell you about the residents of Upton Bay?

3. Why is the novel divided into two parts? How does this structure shape your understanding of the character of Sam? Does Part II change the way you see characters in Part I?

4. Why does Sam end her relationship with J?

5. Discuss the themes of power and victimization in the novel as it relates to: Matias; Samara Lidelsky; Sigrid Johansen; Joan Palmer; Janet Desmond; Irv Randall; Shelley Sommerfeld.

6. How does Sam's perspective change throughout the novel?

7. Discuss the author's choices of names such as Evil Maple Winery and Upton Bay.

8. What is your opinion of Sigrid Johansen, and why?

9. Sam hesitates to call herself a writer early in the novel. When does she change her mind?

10. What does the use of embedded documents and footnotes add to the experience of reading the novel?

Karen Smythe's previous books include the novel *This Side of Sad* (Goose Lane Editions, 2017), the story collection *Stubborn Bones* (Polestar/Raincoast, 2001), and the critical study *Figuring Grief: Gallant, Munro, and the Poetics of Elegy* (McGill-Queen's University Press, 1992). Her family background is Norwegian and German/Irish. She lives with her husband in Guelph, Ontario.